Edit,

THE
GREATEST
ESCAPE

Lou Macaluso

Printed in the United States of America

First Printing August 2019

For Information: Righter's Mill Press
430 Wall Street
Princeton, NJ 08540

Library of Congress Cataloging-Publication-Data
Macaluso, Lou 2-8-1951
The Greatest Escape/Lou Macaluso

ISBN: 978-1-948460-05-7

First Edition

Jacket Designed by Brian Hailes
Visit our Web Site at:
http://www.rightersmill.com

The Greatest Escape

Based on the inspiring true story of the
most daring Cold War exodus.

*Freedom's just another word
for nothin' left to lose.*
—Kris Kristofferson

Acknowledgements

Many thanks to Righters Mill Press and Three Corners Entertainment: Al Longden, my agent/publisher, Jeffrey Batoff, and Karen Venable for believing in me and my work. A special thanks to my editor-mentor-author colleague-literary brother, Richard Sand, for helping make this a better piece of writing, and thus, making me a better writer.

Thanks to Dorinda Urbauer who introduced me to Berlin, German history, and consequently, this story.

Prologue

Thursday, November 9, 1989, 6:00 p.m.

"The sound that you hear and what you are seeing tonight are not hammers and sickles, but hammers and chisels as young people take down this wall bit by bit."

Tom Brokaw speaks those words live from the West Berlin side of the Brandenburg Gate. Behind him, thousands of people, mostly teens and young adults, party by dancing atop the Berlin Wall that once symbolized a harsh separation of Berliners from families, friends, and freedom. East Berlin border guards, once responsible for arresting and killing East Berliners fleeing to freedom, now stand impotent as Germans help each other over the wall and through the chiseled holes. Some guards even drop their weapons and join them.

Timo Fuerst watches the coverage on his TV from the quiet comfort of his living room. He clasps his hands behind his head and feels his thinning hair between his fingers. He remembers how thick curls used to cover his head some thirty years ago when he was a teenager in East Germany. Memories flood through him—memories of loved ones who risked their lives, some successful and many not, escaping from restriction and toward freedom over the past twenty-nine years. He recalls the decision that altered his life forever.

Funny, he thinks and leans forward in his leather recliner chair, *I seem to feel almost nothing. No, not nothing, but a numbness as if many conflicting emotions cancel each other out. The numbness frightens him as he cleans his glasses with the tail of his dress shirt. It's that "quiet before the storm" cliché. He knows that building sensations threaten to overtake him soon.*

Timo has hidden much of his past from his family. Why is that, he wonders? *Is it the result of the East German education that drilled stoicism into me and my classmates during the Cold War? Is it a paternal need to harbor my own sagging emotional load, or would bringing it to the surface uncap a volcanic rush of feelings, and that would embarrass me?*

No, it's more than that. He knows it.

He has kept a pact or a promise within himself all these years. His life has been about following the literal meaning of that East German border guard's words.

"What were those words?" he asks himself. *"Turn away and … run to?"*

He closes his eyes, rocks back on his recliner, and returns to that moment. His subconscious has been storing that image of the guard as if it were a precious piece of film. As he hears the words resonate in his head, his body shakes with all the emotions he has buried deep inside himself.

"Max Thomas, you should have lived to see this day!" he says as if scolding someone in the next room.

PART I:
THE BORDER

Chapter 1

Leipzig, East Germany
Friday, July 28, 1961

Thomas Schleppen & Transport Company. That was the name stenciled on the cab door of the flatbed truck that I backed into the steelyard of Leipzig Structural Steel Company.

"Keep coming, Timo," Max Thomas, my boss, said as he waved me deeper into the yard of high-stacked heavy piles of I-beams, flanges, and web plates.

Max was my hero, eighty-one-years-young. He walked, talked, and carried himself like a man twenty years younger. Time had whitened his hair and slumped his once square, strong shoulders into a more rounded shape, but he moved his six-foot frame like an ambitious young man with purpose in every step. He squinted, not from poor eyesight, but for more clarity into a world that intrigued him. The tense corners of his mouth seemed always ready to smile, laugh, or scream at any moment.

When I was a little boy, I'd sometimes skip school and hang around his hauling company that he ran from his house in our East Berlin suburb, Glienicke/Nordbahn. He had two trucks, a flatbed and a covered trailer. He'd use the trailer for light loads, farm products, gravel, and dirt and the flat bed for heavy loads like these thin but weighty six-meter I-beams the government contracted us to pick up and to deliver to Brandenburg.

I jumped out of the cab after positioning the truck near the beams and joined Max and the steelyard foreman. The foreman, short, stocky and in his late-fifties, ordered his crane operator and material handlers to start loading.

"What's the government want with all these small girders?" asked the foreman.

"Hell, if I know," said Max. "I just sign the invoices and deliver the goods. For all I know that nut, Khrushchev, is building a monument to himself screaming to Western Europe and the United States, 'We will bury you!'"

He took off his shoe and pounded it on a thin steel web plate to mimic the Soviet leader's recent threatening message at the United Nations.

We all laughed.

"Careful, Max," I warned him. "You know how touchy the government has gotten. For a small reward, any one of these company workers could turn you in for speaking treason."

Max smirked as he put his shoe back on. He picked up a stone, hurled it over a thick pile of steel web plates, and said, "No, Timo. That's the sad part of it. They fear rebellion and treason from young people, like you. Old farts like me and Hans," he put his hand on the foreman's shoulder who nodded agreement, "they offer the ultimate humiliation. They ignore us."

As I drove toward Brandenburg, the hum of the diesel engine lulled Max to sleep. I contemplated my life. Sixteen-years-old and my destiny had been mapped out. After ten years of schooling in the *Polytechnische Oberschule*, East German youth had one of the few choices allowed during their lifetime: quit school and go to work or enter vocational training in areas of building, farming, telecommunications, or electronics. After the training, the government assigned you to a collective farm, a factory, or some other government-run institution until your death or you were no longer useful. As much as I yearned to better myself through education, I chose to quit and to work in Max's hauling business. Since the Russians took over half of Germany in the late 40s, freedom lingered inside me. Working for Max was as close to freedom as one could get and still live in East Germany.

We hit a dip in the road along A/9, and the bump awakened Max.

"Where are we?" he asked.

"We're less than an hour from Brandenburg."

Max grabbed the manila folder between us and scanned the invoice papers.

"Does the government say why it needs all these tons of steel crap?" I asked.

An ominous silence followed.

"I don't know. It's written in Russian."

By the time we delivered the steel, the workers unloaded it, and we returned home, it was late at night. All the lights were on at Max's house. It was unusual for Hannah, his wife, to be awake at that hour.

"How about coming in for a beer?" he asked as I pulled the empty flatbed alongside his cottage. This was Max's way of telling me that he considered me a man and not a sixteen-year-old kid. I'd often drink with him and his friends, but I'd never get drunk. Getting drunk might dampen his respect for me, which I cherished. Besides, my sister and her husband who had raised me since my parents' deaths during the war wouldn't allow it.

"No, thanks. I have to work in the morning, and my boss is a grouchy bastard when you show up late."

"You poor slave," he joked and shoved me out the open cab door.

I turned to wave goodbye, but he stood facing his living room as if hesitant to enter.

As I watched him enter his house, the soft rumble of a starting engine turned my attention to a small car passing with its lights off.

We had been followed.

Max remained just inside the doorway and stared across his dimly lit living room and into the passageway of the kitchen. He always appeared much younger in soft light. His erect, lean frame produced the silhouette of a man half his age.

Hannah emerged from the kitchen, leaned against the entranceway, folded her arms, and spoke as if not to awaken a sleeping baby.

"I'm leaving," she said.

"What?"

"I'm leaving," she repeated, uncrossed her arms, and stood straight. Hannah shared Max's quality of looking years younger than her age, but she was already eighteen years Max's junior. In her simple house dress, her shapely figure showed only slight signs of thickening around her hips and shoulders. Greying blond hair hung in a single heavy braid over her shoulder.

A head shorter than her husband, she walked towards him, keeping full eye contact until she positioned herself directly in front of him, looked up, and continued, "I can't take it anymore. I'm crossing over to Frohnau tomorrow and living with Liesel. I can't bear to be away from my daughter and only grandson."

Max raised Liesel as if she were his own. He put his hands on her shoulders as if Hannah were made of glass.

"You see your daughter and little Wolfgang almost daily."

"The border guards make it harder every day, and there's talk of total restriction of East Germans traveling to the West."

"Ahhh, Shit!"

She grabbed Max by the arm, led him through the kitchen, and pointed out the back window and beyond their chicken coop. The border between their East Berlin suburban home and Frohnau, a West Berlin suburb, lay just beyond their backyard. Cars and bicycles could no longer travel down Oranienburger Chaussee, the street that separated the two suburbs. Rolls of barbed wire two meters high stretched the entire length of the road, and guards stood every few kilometers where there were breaks in the barriers for passage.

"Max, open your eyes. They're not just checking passports and asking questions. They're taking passports and making threats. They held my passport this time and told me if I wasn't back within three hours, they would arrest me when I returned and hold my relatives responsible. That's you Max. That means you must come with me."

He walked back out of the kitchen and into the dining area of the huge living room. He sat with his elbows on the dining table and held his head.

West Berlin had been an island of democracy in the middle of Soviet Occupied East Germany after World War II. The West Berlin border, opened for economic trade purposes, became a gateway to freedom for East Germans wanting to escape strict Soviet rule. During the past decade, massive flight had reduced the work force in the East by ten percent. Soviets encouraged the East German government to control travel, and by 1960 all travel from the East to the West had been restricted. Elderly people were allowed short, supervised visits to the West, and Max's hauling business sometimes required him to cross the border for government commerce contracts. Rumors grew that all travel, commercial or not, would soon stop.

Hannah's first husband had worked for him. She was pregnant with their first and only child, Liesel, when he was arrested for being a Jew and sent to the concentration camp in Dachau in 1939 where he died of starvation two years later. Max and Hannah married after the war.

Hannah sat at the opposite end of the dark cherry wood dining table.

They sat in silence for several minutes which must have seemed like hours before he raised his head from his hands, joined his fingers as if in prayer, and spoke, "We'll leave together."

Hannah rose up, but before she could rejoice, he continued, "Give me two weeks to get our affairs together. I need to settle my business matters, gather some equity, and think about a hauling contract that will allow us to smuggle some of our possessions across the border. At our next monthly card club, we can say goodbye to all our friends. Hannah, two weeks is a short time. No one can build a permanent barrier overnight."

She seemed frozen.

Max didn't know if she'd celebrate or protest.

Her mouth widened into a glorious grin. She embraced him and ran to the kitchen where she gathered glasses and retrieved a bottle of *Danziger Goldwasser*.

They sat in the dim light of the dining room and raised their full liqueur flutes.

"To our new life," Hannah toasted.

They couldn't predict the irony of her words and their tragic fate as they clinked glasses.

Chapter 2

Sunday, July 30, 1961

The shock of cold lake water poured onto my sunbaked skin awakened me from a peaceful sleep on our wool blanket. Martina and I had been swimming in Kindel Lake on the northeast border of Glienicke/Nordbahn.

She stood over me with an empty paper cup and a mischievous smile. She wore her shoulder length chestnut hair up whenever we went swimming. Her deep blue eyes, full lips, and short, curvy figure suggested a mature, sexy woman, but her behavior, facial expressions, and speech revealed her true sixteen-year-old, adolescent self. Whenever she cocked her head and bit her lower lip as she was doing then, it was the little girl in the woman's body.

I grabbed her ankle when she tried to run and pulled her on top of me.

"Now, I've got you, and you'll pay for your devious crime."

She laughed and squirmed as I tickled her. Our skirmish ended in a long, passionate kiss. Just as I felt myself being aroused, Martina pushed me to the far end of the blanket and said, "Let's talk."

"Let's not."

I reached for her arm to continue our embrace, but she snapped my wrist away, turned onto her stomach, and said, "We have plenty of time for play."

I rolled onto my back and squinted into the bright afternoon sun. The warming rays dried the dampness from my tight youthful body. Laboring at my job had built tone and definition to my muscles. I hated my thick, brown, curly hair as I forced my fingers through it, front to back, as if that would permanently straighten it. I wanted that stiff, greased-back look of the teen-aged rebels like James Dean and Elvis Presley pictured in the magazines smuggled in from West Berlin.

"Okay, what do you want to talk about?"

"Us. No, let's start with you. What does the future hold for young Timo Fuerst?" She said and pantomimed a fortune teller looking into a crystal ball.

My nervous habit of using my fingers like the teeth of a comb and forcing my hated hair straight back intensified when she revealed the conversation topic. More than my hair, I hated discussing my upcoming plans. My sister and brother-in-law interrogated me almost daily on the subject. The truth was that I had no plans, except to feel the curious sense of freedom when working for a defiant man like Max and having a sensuous girlfriend.

My long silence prompted her to say, "Please tell me it's not working the rest of your life hauling junk for that old man, Max Thomas."

"Why not? It's a solid business. I make a decent wage."

"It's nothing," she said, shut her eyes, and crossed her arms in front of her.

"It's something. I feel a sense of free—"

"It's nothing," she said.

"So, tell me. What is *something*?"

She opened her eyes, turned toward me on her side, and said in a softer tone, "My brother, Olaf."

"*Mein Gott!*"

I turned onto my side, away from her to hide my rolling eyes. Olaf, her older brother, had been training all summer to become part of the East German Border Patrol. In my opinion, Olaf was an arrogant *Dummkopf*—possibly smarter than a rock, but not as bright as a tree.

"Well, *Fräulein* Martina, what about your future?"

Now, she rolled onto her back and peered into the light.

"You know I'll be attending EOS (Extended Secondary School, beyond the compulsory two years of secondary education and only for college bound students) next month with the hope of going to the university in Dresden in two years."

My question was somewhat rhetorical. I knew she would be going to EOS, and I knew she had talked about doing medical training at the university. But I wasn't prepared for the most recent addition to her plan.

"But I'll let you in on my latest idea."

Noises across the lake bounced off the still water.

We sat up and supported ourselves on our elbows.

"I hope to meet a handsome, ambitious young man. Some successful person who will give me prestige and buy me anything I want."

Nearby a small group of couples, laughed and shed their clothes before splashing into the cool, clear lake. Nudism had become popular in East Germany. Later, psychologists would theorize that it provided a feeling of freedom and escape for people confined within a communist society.

"And how in this communist state do you plan to do that? The only men who rise to fame and fortune are military officers and political figures."

"You've just answered your own question."

"Holy hell."

"What's wrong with being a soldier or a leader?"

Two couples swam away from the others and toward a small grassy island in the middle of the lake.

"They are puppets, just humans dancing on strings to the tune of someone else. One wears a uniform and the other a suit."

Martina stood and stared at the island. She was seductive in her tight-fitting, one-piece bathing suit. The bikini had become popular in western cultures but was considered risqué in eastern bloc countries. She ran to the edge, dove, and remained underwater for some time.

The noisy, frolicking nudists only reminded me of my growing sexual tension. Martina and I had experimented with our lovemaking, but we were both virgins.

Her head emerged above the surface of the deep water where her underwater swim had taken her, and she waved for me to join her.

Her one-piece suit floated toward the shoreline.

I kicked off my trunks and entered the lake. She pretended to swim away from me but allowed me to catch her by her calves and pull her into a long embrace. Her eyes closed, and her lips parted when she felt my erection grow between her thighs. The consummation of our lust had come in the most perfect place for inexperienced lovers. Water provided an excuse for our clumsiness but didn't deter the ecstasy of that first time.

We walked home in silence.

"How do you feel?" asked Martina when we reached her house.

I wanted to say "triumphant," but that sounded boastful, maybe even offensive.

"Relieved and happy, you?"

She paused a moment and stared at her front door. Her family lived on the bottom floor of a two-flat. Most of the world would describe it as modest at best. East Germans considered it a luxury duplex. Her parents worked at a distributing plant for Vita Cola, the East's rival to Coca Cola. Most working-class East Germans lived in drab, sterile housing projects. Every apartment looked the same: one bedroom, one bath. But the reward for having children was better housing and free daycare. Martina's family fit the mold of the perfect communist household—two working parents and two children, a boy and a girl.

I waited like an Olympic athlete, anticipating the judges' scores. Every young man wants to think he is a virile and great lover, or at worst, much better than just adequate.

Her eyes turned toward the sky. She grinned, pirouetted, kissed me on the cheek, and said, "Glorious. I feel like a full woman, and guess what? Every Sunday my parents will be in Brandenburg visiting my father's aunt. And guess what, again?"

This time she waited for an answer.

"What?"

She opened the door, took both my hands as if they might break, led me into the living room, and said, "Today is Sunday."

I clasped her hands and stopped when I looked beyond her.

We were not alone.

Chapter 3

An East German border guard in full uniform stood up from the dining room table in the main first floor room. He removed his visor cap with the signature green band and centered metallic emblem. His stone-grey uniform had a thick brown leather belt worn between the ribcage and waist that tailored the jacket. The open collar of his light grey dress shirt and his loosened dark tie expressed a slight suggestion of informality.

He didn't look much older than I, but we couldn't have looked more different. His straight blond hair, chiseled facial features, and erect posture reminded me of a flyer my sister kept in a trunk along with pictures of our parents and various Nazi and World War II paraphernalia. It depicted a muscular young man wearing a brown shirt and tie and raising the Nazi flag. The handbill touted him as the ideal Nazi, an example of the Aryan or the "master race."

The border guard seemed a little embarrassed as he attempted an introduction. Olaf, holding a full beer stein in each hand, interrupted when he appeared in the living room doorway, spread his arms, and announced, "I'm home!"

Martina raced toward him and hugged him around his neck.

He leaned forward and accepted the embrace, but didn't hug back, probably in fear of spilling the drinks. His round, chubby face and stout, short physique contrasted in almost every way with the other young man's appearance. Their only common feature was their blond hair, although Olaf's receding hairline foreshadowed early baldness. He hadn't changed much after a summer of military training. The only difference was his eyewear. He had entered the guard school wearing popular-for-the-time black-rimmed glasses. Retro style frames, dark plastic tops with wire bottoms, now supported his thick lenses. "Timo, I'm glad you're here. I've got something for you," said Olaf. "Both of you sit down."

He set the steins on the table near his friend and dashed back into the kitchen. The fact that he had left his friend standing there like an idiot without an introduction didn't surprise me.

I thought he had returned to the kitchen to get beverages for Martina and me, but he came back with a handful of literature, two booklets and a pamphlet with the same theme—*A Glorious Career in the East German Border Guards.*

Martina punched me under the table.

"Thank you, Olaf,"

My tone of voice couldn't have been more lifeless, but he just gloated, patted me on the shoulder, and didn't pick up on the sarcasm.

"Oh, sorry, I forgot. Martina, Timo, this is my friend, Christian. He's been assigned to border patrol in our neighborhood. Let's raise our glasses and toast to him."

"Olaf, you and your friend have beer, but you didn't bring anything for Timo and me to drink," said Martina.

"Oh, sorry again. Well, just pretend. To Christian, —A glorious career in the East German border guards."

So, we raised our imaginary glasses in imaginary congratulations.

"Have they assigned you to our local border, too, Olaf?" I asked.

He took a long draught from his beer before answering and almost forgot to swallow before speaking.

"No, Timo," Olaf said as if educating an infant on a well-known phenomenon. "Guards are not assigned to their hometowns. I leave for Boeckwitz tomorrow."

"Where are you from, Christian?" asked Martina.

"Potsdam," Christian answered.

"Our class received our assignments on Friday," Olaf added. "When I heard Christian was assigned to Glienicke/Nordbahn, I invited him for dinner. I forgot that Mom and Dad would be out of town. Martina, could you see if there is something to prepare?"

Martina distorted her face into a frown and went to the kitchen.

"Tell me," I asked both, "why don't they allow border guards to work in their hometowns?"

"Just to make things easier, so nothing is personal in case there are arguments or fights," Christian answered and drank from his mug.

"What kind of arguments or fights occur? I mean, we have free but limited access to travel across the border now. What problems come up?"

Olaf and Christian looked at each other. They seemed to share a secret, and my naïve questioning challenged their keeping it. Olaf started to answer, but Christian interrupted him.

"Timo, you know travelers from our side must produce a passport and tell us why they want to cross the border before being assigned a time limited visit in the West."

I nodded.

"Well, noncompliance means denial to cross and that often causes disagreements which can result in arrests."

I waited for both to drink some more beer before I asked, "Let's say the person resists arrest and bolts for the border?"

"We shoot them," said Olaf with a smile.

His answer startled me, and I sat up straight in my chair. Up until then, arrests for defection were many and punishments harsh, but if deaths occurred, they were few.

"You could do that, Olaf? You could kill someone?" I asked.

He nodded and kept smiling.

"We must," said Christian without emotion or a facial expression. He seemed almost like a mannequin, a perfectly molded being: crisp, cut, and combed blond hair, blue eyes—cold blue eyes.

I wondered if military training had hardened a once sensitive boy or if he ever harbored a soul. A strange feeling crept within me. Maybe it was the insecurity we all experience when growing up. He didn't frighten me, but he seemed to challenge something inside me. *Was I less of a man because I wasn't a military man*, I wondered?

"So, Timo, what is your occupation?" Christian asked.

Before I could speak, Olaf answered as if he were giving the punchline to a joke, "He's a hauler."

No one laughed, but Christian twisted his face into a confused expression.

Olaf seemed to want to explain, but I wouldn't let him.

"Be quiet, Olaf," I said and turned to Christian. "We transport all kinds of things: produce, farm equipment, building materials. Nearly all our work is contracted by the government."

Christian put his elbow on the table, stroked his chin, and said, "Ah, I see. So, you are working to build your country and the state in some capacity."

"I guess you could say that."

"Excellent," Christian said and leaned toward me as he asked, "but don't you think you could better serve—"

Martina's voice from the kitchen cut him off.

"There's enough chicken in the refrigerator for me to put a dinner together. Timo, are you staying?"

"No," I said and stood, "I'll be leaving. It was good to meet you, Christian."

He raised himself as if called to attention, reached over the table, and shook my hand. His handshake was firm and formal. It surprised me that we were the same height. He had seemed taller from afar.

As I turned toward the front door, Olaf said, "Don't forget your stuff."

I smiled and retrieved the *A Glorious Career in the East German Border Guards* propaganda.

Martina joined me, and we walked out together. Once the door closed behind us, I heard myself say, "Well, it looks like you found that military man in your plan."

She looked at me with astonishment and punched me in my upper arm.

"Don't be stupid. I was only teasing back then." She caressed the same arm she had just hit and said, "Timo is my soldier."

We kissed for a long time before she said, "When will I see you again?"

"I'll be working all this week, but if I get home early enough, I'll come by whenever I can at night."

"Don't forget about our Sundays now."

"How can I?"

She returned inside.

I cut through the city park on my way home. The late summer sun had already set, and the benches, weeping willow trees, and greenery along the dirt path darkened. I thought about my own paths: my social life, my family, my work. Yes, my work, so routine. That would change in the next several hours.

I tossed the border guard literature into a garbage can.

Chapter 4

Monday, July 31, 1961

I slammed the grey, drab door of our grey, drab third floor apartment that I shared with my sister and brother-in-law at around 6:15 that morning. This routine seldom varied every weekday and sometimes on Saturday when I left for work.

My eyes avoided the bleak buildings as I walked through town. There were plenty of colorless, cheerless high-rise housing projects in East Berlin, but only a few in Glienicke/Nordbahn. Before it became part of the Soviet communist sector in 1949, Glienicke/Nordbahn had been considered an upscale community. The Marxist movement to make every person and every place the same meant scaling down the suburb's prestige. Building these cheap, sterile apartments helped the movement.

Except for sleeping on the sofa of our single-bedroom-single-bath apartment, I spent my time away and alone with my thoughts either at Max and Hannah's place, with Martina, or in the park. Sometimes I even slept beneath a tree or on a park bench.

As usual, I entered the Thomas cottage from the front door. Max and his longtime friend, Sven Engel, sat at the dining table drinking coffee and laughing. Sven, in his seventies, could have passed for Max's kid brother. Shorter and much thinner than Max, they had a mutual youthful exuberance for life. Sven had a full crop of greyish/white hair which he kept hidden under a faded green flat cap. His typical attire included a blue cotton work shirt, sleeves rolled halfway up his forearms, and washed-out chinos cuffed at the ankle. An unbuttoned grey formal vest offset his workingman appearance but complemented his offbeat sense of humor.

The retired wise-cracking electrician worked with us off and on. He knew the hauling business, top to bottom, so if Max was ever sick or injured, which was not often, Sven could step right in and keep things going.

As soon as they saw me enter, they stopped laughing and gave each other a sobering stare.

"What are you perverted old men cackling about?" I asked.

"You," Sven said and adjusted his cap front and back, his signature habit before mocking. "We were picturing you making love to that little girlfriend of yours." He took off his cap, wrapped a cloth napkin around his head, and continued in a high-pitched female voice, "Oh, Timo, you're such a stud horse. Don't stop. One more time."

Max winced. He was so amused he could hardly breathe.

Hannah entered with a mug of coffee for me and said, "Are they making fun of you again, Timo? Leave my boy alone."

She hugged me, and I wrapped her arms around my neck in acknowledgment. She, too, was in gleeful spirits.

"Does he know?"

Her question brought the two men back to a more serious mood. Whatever had made all of them so happy before I arrived must have been a secret—a secret they weren't sure about sharing.

"You must tell him sometime," she said. "It affects him, and he is part of the plan."

Max moved his chair closer to me. He put his heavy, calloused hand on my shoulder and said, "Hannah and I are leaving. We're defecting to the West in a few weeks."

The chemistry of emotions—fear, anger, happiness, bewilderment—had never passed through my mind and body with such a rush before this. My face either flushed or grew pale, but something felt strange as my jaws quivered and the words stuttered from my mouth.

"But why? How?" I said and ran my fingers through my hair.

"Don't worry, Timo. You'll still have a job. Sven will take over the business, and in a few years, if you're still interested, the business will be yours."

Sven smiled and nodded.

"Visitation restrictions are getting tighter every day, and there's talk of stopping all travel to the West. Hannah can't live without her daughter and grandson, and I can't live without Hannah."

The silence seemed to last forever.

Then all at once it hit me. These people I loved so much would be free and happy, and I would have the hauling business.

"*Mein Gott*," I laughed and hugged them both, "I will miss you two."

All four of us toasted with our coffee mugs.

"Now, let's all sit down," said Sven who appeared to take charge. "First," he pointed at me, "you are to tell no one. Understood?"

Insulted that he even questioned my confidence and loyalty, I grimaced and waved him off.

"I'm serious, Timo. I know you wouldn't want to, but sometimes people slip."

Realizing his seriousness, I nodded with emphasis.

"Now, listen carefully to the plan. It is so simple it is almost funny. That's really what we were laughing at when you came in. They'll leave two weeks from today."

It was Monday. Every Monday *Thomas Schleppen & Transport Company* had a standing government contract to cross over to Frohnau for a half day. A huge farmer's market took place on weekends there, all year round. Before the East-West split of Berlin and its suburbs, the farmers from our town participated in it. Now, they were forbidden, but the

Soviets had a contract to buy up all the leftover, unsold products at a flat fee. Farmers used some as feed for livestock, and the rest was sold to us in grocery stores. The plan became obvious to me. The border guards were used to seeing any combination of Max, Sven, and me when they checked our papers before crossing. We would hide Max and Hannah, so they wouldn't need to be accounted for on the return. But that left a huge problem. We always entered Frohnau with an empty covered trailer. The guard always inspected it and the cab.

"Are we taking them when we make the Monday market run?"

"I told you he was a smart kid," Max said to Sven.

"But how—"

"Will we sneak them across?" Sven finished my question. "Follow us."

We walked outside to the truck trailer. Sven worked the metal latch of the back doors and opened them.

"They'll hide right there."

It was completely empty—nowhere to hide, nothing to hide behind. I jumped inside and inspected. I thought maybe they could hide under the floorboards, but I could see the ground through splintered spaces between the planks.

Max and Sven set down their cups and climbed inside. Max kicked in a corner of the back wall and Sven pulled the other side. It was a false wall. When in place it allowed about a three-foot space between it and the real back wall of the trailer. They had installed I-hooks on the inside of the false wall for someone in the created space to latch it tightly into place.

"Old magicians' trick I learned as a kid. Over the weekend, while you were probably either deflowering your little girlfriend or pleasuring yourself, we 'perverted old men,' as you referred to Max and me, installed it."

I put my arms over their shoulders and said, "Yes, my wise elders, but will it work?"

"We'll find out," said Max.

"When?" I asked.

"Now," said Sven, and he gulped down the rest of his coffee.

The truck engine sounded like a grumbling beast as Sven and I sat in the cab and waited in line to clear customs before entering Frohnau, West Berlin district. The East German border guards seemed to take more time than usual checking documents and searching vehicles. Two commercial flatbed trucks idled in front of us. From the driver's side window, I looked south down Oranienburger Chaussee, the border. I could see Max and Hannah's backyard. Hannah crouched behind the chicken coop and pretended to garden. Her real focus was on us.

Max had sealed himself inside the three-foot hiding space. It was essential that someone be there to fasten the eye-hooks from inside the false wall. Otherwise, the rumbling truck ride might jar the wall loose. They allowed a truck through the crossing gate and now only one flatbed stood in front of us.

Leipziger Strasse was the only border crossing north of the East Berlin city limits. It occurred to me that if this border station closed, there would be no way to enter the West from Glienicke/Nordbahn.

A problem emerged. The border crossing guard yelled at the driver. Several more guards arrived on the scene. They searched the cab and the trailer like burglars looking for cash. We didn't know what had transpired, but it ended with the driver being cuffed and arrested, and a guard drove the truck away.

The border guard motioned for me to drive forward toward the gate. Sven rolled down his window, and the guard jumped onto the running board and said, "Documents and passports, please."

With a wide grin, Sven adjusted his cap and handed him our standard packet including passports, invoice, and government permission forms and said, "Glorious morning, isn't it? Having a rough day?"

I hated when he did this. Sven had an innate distaste for authority. He also had a wit as sharp as a surgical knife. He used humor to get under his prey's skin. The problem? East German border guards were humorless.

The guard ignored him and examined the papers.

"I love the hats you guys wear. That green band and the badge in front. Aren't they great, Timo?"

"Yes," I said in a low, quiet voice. I turned away from him, pretended to stare out the window, and combed my hair with my fingers. I didn't know whether to shake with laughter or tremble from fear.

"Out, both of you."

As he made a thorough inspection of the cab, Sven said, "No, really, where can I get a hat like that?"

The guard stepped down from the running board and looked down upon the much shorter Sven.

"You have to be a member of The East German Border Patrol. Sorry, old man, I think that time has passed you by. Now, follow me," he said and marched toward the rear of the trailer and inspected beneath it.

Every time he looked forward, Sven mimicked his stiff military gate.

When two other guards spotted his mockery, I thought we were in trouble, but they just snickered and turned away.

"Open the doors," the guard said to me.

He clambered inside and stepped to the middle. The morning sun illuminated the back end of the trailer, but darkness concealed the rear trailer wall. With the beam of his flashlight, he inspected every centimeter of the floor, ceiling, side walls, and, last, the back wall. He seemed fixated on that back wall. Had he heard Max in there? Did he suspect the wall to be false? All he had to do was fire a line of bullets across that wall with his automatic weapon to address any such suspicions.

"Hey," said Sven, "I should have told you. Our last hauling job was livestock. Be careful. I wouldn't want you to get goat shit on your shiny brown boots."

He darted the light toward his feet, then pivoted on his heels, and stomped toward us.

"Fuck off! Get going, you silly old fart, and be back before two o'clock!" He threw our papers and crossing permit at us but held our passports.

We gathered the papers, hopped into the cab, and drove across the border without even closing the trailer doors.

Chapter 5

Sunday, August 6, 1961

Horst read the Sunday edition of *Neues Deutschland* as we sipped our coffee and waited for Frieda to prepare a less than hearty breakfast of hard, stale rolls, cheese, cold cuts that had started to harden on the edges, and soupy oatmeal. We couldn't escape being together on Sunday mornings. They didn't work that day, and I routinely overslept.

"They'll be hiring at our factory soon" said Horst from behind his paper shield. "Interested?"

"You don't know that," Frieda said as she stirred oatmeal in a bowl at the counter. Frieda's short, black/greying hair stuck out at greasy angles, and her obese body moved with a slight limp in her old flannel robe.

A sting of guilt ran through me whenever I spoke negatively about Frieda. I owed her much. Sixteen years older than I, she raised me when our parents died during an air strike that hit the paper factory where they worked. We lived in Berlin then but moved to this near northern suburb when she married Horst a few years later.

A few old photos from the rotting steamer trunk she kept in their bedroom showed a plain but happy teen-aged Frieda posing with my parents in front of our old house and another at a picnic. One would never have recognized anything similar about that gangling young girl with the long black hair and this woman. Gravity seemed to work more on Frieda than everyone else. It pulled at her loose rolls of skin and forced her to drag her feet when she walked. Only in her mid-thirties, she looked decades older.

"I know more than you think."

Frieda turned from her stirring and flashed a quizzical look.

"Kurt shared a secret after a few beers last night. He and Erna have been saving up. They're defecting to West Berlin at the end of the month."

Frieda's expression changed to rage. She took her wooden spoon and slapped him on the side of the head, and sticky oatmeal splattered and stuck to his balding head above the ear.

"Shithead!" she said in a low, hissing voice. "These thin walls. Anyone can hear you. If the Stasi knew that you knew and didn't report it, they'd punish us worse than them."

Horst scraped the oatmeal from his head and flung it back at her when she turned away. He was a caricature of himself, a stereotyped grumpy German worker. His bald head, stubbly beard, red face, and beer belly protruding out of a stained and torn tank t-shirt made him look like one of the colorful comic strip characters from the only section of the newspaper that he understood well. Scratching himself in public surprised no one who knew his crude behaviors.

He scraped his dirty fingernails across his belly, directed his attention back to the newspaper, and said, "Well, my question still stands. Interested in a job at our plant?"

I shook my head. Even though he wasn't looking at me, he knew my stock answer.

"Didn't think so," he said. "He'd rather work with old man Max. No ambition. *Nichts.*"

Here we go again, I thought. If I wasn't getting needled by Martina about my life, I was getting lectured by these two. At least with Martina, our discussions often ended in lovemaking. With my sister and brother-in-law, conversations evolved into arguments. My only defense was to keep my answers short and my presence shorter.

"Here," he said and tossed the classified section toward me. "Improve your mind and maybe your life."

"Stop. It's too early to start fighting," said Frieda and plopped two bowls of gooey oatmeal in front of us. "Eat your breakfast." Frieda and Horst tolerated my existence and welcomed my rent money, but they complained about everything else: their factory jobs, their lack of children, their lack of decent housing because of their lack of children, and so on, and so on. No doubt that they had spent a typical Saturday night at a beer hall. Horst drank too much, and Frieda would get drunk just to spite him. They would argue all night until they both passed out.

I rinsed my bowl and coffee cup and headed for the door.

"That's right," said Horst. "Eat and run. No time to be sociable. No time for family."

The irony was that they no more wanted me around than I desired to be with them. Sometimes on Sundays, they tried to be a happy, married couple. Frieda packed a picnic basket, and they drove their two-stroke engine car, a Trabant, to the country for a quiet, romantic interlude. One or both would drink too much which ignited another battle and ended with them going to work Monday morning, tired, hungover, and ready to repeat another cycle of their pathetic lives.

Although clouds blocked much of the sunlight, the park seemed radiant and lively on my way to see Martina. Maybe it was just thinking about me making love to her, picturing the freedom and happiness in store for Max and Hannah, or dreaming about the prospect of owning and running Max's company. Of course, my plan would be interrupted by eighteen months of compulsory military service when I turned eighteen, but I would endure it while Sven ran the hauling business. Besides, even though I would hate the military uniform and life, it impressed Martina.

Just before stepping onto the paved path that led out of the park, two heavy hands landed on my shoulders and a deep male voice said, "Not so fast Timo Fuerst. We need to talk."

I turned and faced him.

Chapter 6

My eyes looked upward at the tall young man in the tailored brown suit. Something looked familiar about him, but I couldn't place him. Perhaps ten years older than I, his thin blond hair receded like Olaf's, but, no, he didn't look at all like Olaf. His thick lips seemed to be pouting, but it was his eyes that struck me as reminiscent of someone else.

"How do you know my name, and who—"

He reached into his pocket and flashed identification that answered my questions. Similar to a passport, the booklet opened to a small circular silver badge on one side and a photo ID on the other—his signature and a stamped last name next to his picture. I couldn't make out his faintly imprinted name or his scrawling signature, but the bold-faced words above were clear: *Ministerium fur Staatssicherheit*. Better known as the Stasi, it represented the major intelligence and secret police agency in East Germany. The Stasi, headquartered in East Berlin, carried out many tasks, but its main duties were spying on the population, rooting out dissenters, and punishing them. The KGB maintained liaison officers with each Stasi sector. In short, you didn't mess with the Stasi.

He replaced a hand on my shoulder, this time with a light touch, and spoke in a softer tone.

"Let's sit down on a bench and talk," he said and led me back onto the dirt path and into the park.

I felt myself start to perspire and couldn't figure what he wanted with me.

"Relax, Timo. You're not in any trouble. If you were, I would have arrested you already, and you would be off to Siberia." He laughed, lit a cigarette, and continued. "Want a smoke?"

I shook my head and tried to speak without quivering. "So, then, what is it you want?"

He blew out a rich cloud of grey smoke and sighed with pleasure.

"Ah, I love German parks. Don't you, Timo? So peaceful. That weeping willow tree over there that you often sleep under to get out of the drunken noise of your sister and brother-in-law's warring. Yes, we know a lot about you, Timo. Does that upset you?"

"Not really," I answered because it didn't surprise me that the Stasi knew so much about any East German citizen. Their reputation for spying even on innocent people was notorious, and I didn't feel I had anything to hide.

"My reason for talking with you is actually a good one. You see, my younger brother, Christian, seemed quite impressed by you."

The resemblance hit me. The eyes. He and Christian had the same cold blue eyes, but this man's eyes appeared even colder.

"I only met your brother once, and he didn't mention a brother by name—"

"My name is of no importance to you—just my position. I'm an agent of the Ministry of State Security, Administration 2000. We're in charge of recruitment for NVA, *Nationale Volksarmee* (National People's Army)."

The National People's Army reported their neighbors for anti-Soviet actions and words. I called them German traitors. Another faction of the Stasi handled punishments for subversion, which could be anything from a warning, to imprisonment, to torture or even death.

"You mean you want me to spy on people like my boss? I can tell you there's no finer man than Max Thomas, and he'd never—"

Christian's nameless brother laughed.

"No, no, we're not interested in old worthless people like Max Thomas and his ancient, card playing friends. Although some of our more zealous but not very bright NVA insist on following such people."

This reminded me of Max's words a few days before: "They offer the ultimate humiliation. They ignore us." It also reminded me of the car that followed us that day.

"What we're interested in is recruiting smart youth like yourself, youth, anxious to get ahead in this world and smart enough to keep us informed for the sake of reward."

I stared straight ahead and refused to take the bait. His comment begged the questions: What information? What reward? But I remained silent.

"We're also interested in your sister, your brother-in-law, and the plant where they work."

Now he had my attention, and I couldn't help but blurt out, "Are you serious? Frieda and Horst? You think you know so much about people? When they're not working, they're either too drunk, too lazy, or too stupid to do anything but sleep, fight, or get drunker."

He nodded and seemed to be suppressing another laugh.

"We're aware of all that, Timo. Strangely, it's their drunken nature that we're counting on. They, particularly your brother-in-law, tend to be very talkative when they get drunk. Rumors of something going on within the plant have reached us, but we don't know what: sabotage, defection, maybe nothing."

My face flushed when I thought of Horst's announcement that morning of the couple who planned to defect at the end of the month. I ran my fingers through my hair and shook my head.

"I don't know anything, and if I did learn something, what makes you think I want to be responsible for someone tortured or killed?"

"Timo, Timo," he smiled and put his hand on my shoulder again. "You're too impressed with the Stasi. We're not barbarians. We wouldn't hurt anyone. All I ask is that you keep your ears open. If you hear anything, tell me."

"How would I find you?"

"Don't worry. I'll find you. Now, enjoy the day. Go visit that little girlfriend of yours. I understand her parents are away for the day."

He flashed a mischievous smile, flicked his cigarette across the path into the wet grass, and left.

I sat and reviewed what had just happened. A red squirrel near the trunk of a willow tree seemed to be watching me. It ran up the tree and disappeared behind the weeping willow branches. After about twenty minutes, I came to a comforting conclusion. I would forget this encounter with Christian's brother and take pleasure in my Sunday with Martina.

"Has it started to rain, yet?" asked Martina.

I turned my head on the pillow and looked through the lace covering the window in her bedroom. "I can't tell. I'll get up and open the curtains."

"No," she said and pulled me closer to her. "Don't leave. I like the way your warm body feels against mine."

We had made love, and we were both exhausted and euphoric. Our eyes closed, and we enjoyed the tranquil silence while raindrops tapped on the window. Martina's soft voice interrupted my half sleep.

"You've been unusually happy lately."

"I've been making love with the most beautiful girl in Glienicke/ Nordbahn."

"No, I mean all week, when you came for dinner on Wednesday, at Tanja's party last night. What happened? Did old man Max Thomas give you a raise? Give you his business?"

"Something like that."

She turned her body and faced me.

"What?"

I had almost told her, but Sven's words came back to me, "You are to tell no one ... I know you wouldn't want to, but sometimes people slip." I stood up and went to the window. It was starting to rain harder.

"It's just a change in my state of mind."

She giggled.

"What's so funny?"

"You. 'State of mind.' Olaf talks about having a Soviet state of mind. He says you don't have it."

I sat on the bed, continued to watch the rain, and said, "He's probably right, but what is a Soviet state of mind?"

"I'm not sure, but I think it means literally living for the Soviet state. Being content that you work hard for your Soviet state, that you have children for the Soviet state, that you live for the Soviet state."

"And what about a German state of mind?" I turned and faced her. "What about our country?"

She sat up. "Face it, Timo. Germany is broken. We've been sliced up and destroyed by the Allies and the Soviets. Our history shattered by Nazi lies and immoral acts."

"I'm not talking about Nazi Germany or even our land cut up into pieces. I'm talking about our German way of life, our culture, our freedom—that's a state of mind."

"You're hopelessly romantic, my love," she said and pulled the cover up to her neck.

"What does that mean?" I asked and stared out the window again.

"It means you don't see things factually. You're impractical, a dreamer."

"What's wrong with that?"

"Nothing. It's something I love about you, but your dreams can only come true if you adapt them to the real world. Otherwise, they just exist in your head, in a dream world."

A question had been gnawing inside me ever since Martina and I had that conversation at the lake about our future dreams. I hadn't asked it because I feared her answer. The darkness in the room offered me a certain confidence—maybe because it's just words penetrating the blackness without misinterpreted gestures, facial expressions, or reactions. I turned, sat on the windowsill, and thought for several moments before speaking.

"In this *real* world," I said, "what would be your dream for me?"

The room's dim obscurity allowed me to imagine her sitting up and exposing her seductive breasts. She spoke as if her answer had been rehearsed.

"You follow my brother's advice and become a border guard—no, not just a border guard, but the best border guard. You become an officer, maybe even a general. We marry, begin a large family, and move to the finest house in a big city like East Berlin or even Moscow. If we tire of that or find military life doesn't suit us, you use your service record to enter politics, you become a high-ranking administrative official in East Germany or maybe even at the Kremlin."

Chapter 7

Saturday, August 5, 1961

Such a beautiful night to sleep in the park. The weeping willow draped over me like a canopy. Thick grass as a mattress and my crumpled shirt for a pillow made up my natural bed. The sky looked like a distant city with tiny lights poking through the darkness.

I thought about my date with Martina. There wasn't much for teens to do in Glienicke/Nordbahn on a Saturday night. We had a local movie theater, but most East German movies had a Soviet political message woven into them. Theaters could only show films made in Eastern bloc countries such as Poland, Czechoslovakia, or Russia. Every few months, rumors spread that an underground copy of a popular Western Europe or USA film circulated in East Berlin. That summer everyone talked about the James Dean film, *Rebel Without a Cause*. The East German government in association with the Soviet Union published an article in *Neues Deutschland* admonishing the film as Western propaganda promoting rebellious anarchy among the youth. They urged citizens to report any knowledge of the showing or illegal distribution of it in East Germany.

That night, *Kino Glienicke*, our movie theater, featured *The Silent Star*. The plot involved some scientists or engineers accidentally discovering a mysterious "spool" in the Gobi Desert. It's 1985, and somehow the "spool" leads them to the planet Venus and an alien conspiracy to blow up earth with atomic bombs. I didn't watch much of it, because the universal purpose of all teenage movie dates was to kiss and to pet in the dark.

Martina's parents enforced an eleven thirty curfew. We didn't mind that anymore since their ritual visits to Brandenburg provided a place for our Sunday matinee lovemaking. We held hands, walked back to her house via the park, and fantasized about our sexual adventures for the following day.

"Timo, why do you always walk so slowly when we cut through the park?'

"I don't know. I love parks. They're peaceful and calming."

As we approached the park bench near the end of the path, my meeting with Christian's brother came to mind and a chill ran through me. I reminded myself not to think about that and all his Stasi espionage talk.

"To me they're spooky, especially at night. Is that why you sleep in parks so much?"

"Partly," I said and left it at that. It was more than that. It was personal. Parks were not my second home. They *were* my home. Living in a dinky apartment with two drunks and sleeping on a cheap, lumpy couch couldn't be called home. The soft summer breezes blowing through the trees replaced the lullabies my mother sang to me as a child, and the chirping birds provided the alarm clock I needed as an adult.

Thinking about Martina and our evening while lying under that tree in the park, made my dream world more genuine. My city in the sky became real, and my body became dreamlike. I drifted up through the willow branches toward the stars. Max and Hannah floated above me in the same direction. They accelerated higher and higher. I seemed to stop moving upward. Martina held my feet and urged me to return to earth. "Come with me," I pleaded, but she remained and let me go. Her image got smaller and smaller as I rose higher and higher toward the lights as if a huge balloon pulled me skyward. Just before catching up to Max and Hannah, my imaginary balloon must have burst. I descended toward earth at a sure fatal speed. I looked below for Martina, but she wasn't there. Olaf and Christian dressed in full guard uniforms watched and laughed.

A jarring sensation awakened me. Sunlight seeped through the low-hanging willow branches. It must have been several hours past dawn. Horst had been shaking my shoulders.

"I've been looking all over for you. Come quick. Something terrible has happened."

I followed him to his car, and we sped off.

Horst didn't speak during the short ride back to our apartment building. His disheveled appearance, the stale alcohol stench in the car, and his erratic driving indicated he was still intoxicated from the night before. Every time I'd ask what happened, he'd just sputter in a hushed voice as if he were afraid anyone but me might hear, "Bastards."

As if by instinct, my legs took three stairs at a time up the stairwell to the apartment while Horst labored behind me. The door opened to a catastrophic mess. It looked like a whirlwind had magically spewed and then vanished in the middle of the apartment. All the furniture in the living room and kitchen had been overturned. Someone had opened every cabinet and drawer, and all the contents covered the floor which left half the dishes and glassware broken. Some person or persons had made the effort to take all the food and drink from the refrigerator and smashed it against the walls and floor.

Frieda's whimpering drew me into the bedroom. Except for the bed, which she and Horst must have taken the time to reinstate to its original place, the room looked in the same condition as the rest of the apartment. The dresser drawers were opened, and clothes scattered everywhere.

"What happened, Frieda?" I asked after taking her hand into mine. It had been years since I had felt any affection or pity for my sister. She and

Horst had built a wall between us, so that no love or kind feeling linked us, just an obligation to respect a brother and sister relationship in reverence to our deceased parents. Now I felt, if not pity or love, a deep concern.

She sat up in bed with her stained, flannel robe covering her upper body and the blanket pulled to her waist. With an ice bag on her head, she just whimpered with her eyes closed and her cheeks tearstained.

"Go ahead. Tell him. Just like you told me," Horst said and stood in the doorway.

She opened her eyes and smiled at me. It reminded me of when she was young, pretty, and had shown some affection for her younger brother.

"Oh, Timo, Timo, it was awful," she said and closed her eyes again.

"Come on. I want to hear it again, too," Horst said. He came closer but offered no comfort or consolation.

She sighed, removed the ice bag from her head, and opened her eyes wide before speaking. Her contempt for Horst's lack of compassion seemed to compose her, and her usual sarcastic tone crept into her voice.

"I was sitting by myself in the beer hall because Horst, of course, left me so he could joke with his drinking buddies at another table. A couple with a pitcher of beer came over to my table and sat down, she on one side and he on the other."

"Who cares who sat where? Get to what happened," Horst said and sat on the end of the bed with his head in his hands.

"They said I looked lonely, and the man filled my mug from his pitcher. He was bald, young looking, short, with thick, meaty arms and his work shirt sleeves rolled all the way up. She wore a simple house dress like the one I wear at work, but it didn't look right on her. She looked too prim and proper to be wearing it. It looked like a costume on her.

"We talked, and they seemed like a nice couple. They said they worked in a tool and die factory nearer to Brandenburg and hadn't been to this beer hall before. Then they started asking about my job and where

I worked. They told me they heard rumors about someone or some people working at our plant who were planning something against the state. I told them I hadn't heard anything, but they didn't seem to believe me.

"After some time, they changed the subject and kept ordering more pitchers of beer. The woman said she needed some fresh air and asked if I'd join her outside for a smoke."

"And you, like a *Dummkopf,* went with her."

Frieda ignored Horst's comment and continued, "We went out front, lit up, and everything seemed normal. Then the man came out, grabbed me by the arm, and they both dragged me to the alley behind the beer hall. She stood in the passageway between buildings and watched for passersby. He ripped my dress open and said, "Now, tell me what's going on in your factory.'

"I told him I didn't know what he meant. That's when he put his hand into my underpants and stuck his finger inside me and said, 'Next, time it won't be my finger. It will be something more painful.' He turned me around. I felt a thump on the back of my head, and that's the last thing I remember."

Horst was crying as he said, "I went looking for her about an hour later. Found her lying in the alley. Covered her up and brought her home to this."

I stood up, marched in front of Horst, and said, "You fool! Why didn't you go to the police? Or—"

The absurdity of my question hit me. *In a sense, it was the police. The police were just a puppet of the Stasi, and the Stasi was behind the assault.*

"Never mind," I said, patted Horst on the shoulder, and entered the living room like a zombie. There was a lot to think about. I turned the sofa upright, sat, and tried to make sense of everything, but my mind went numb.

Only one person was of sober mind and spirit to take charge of the apartment—me. I spent hours cleaning. By late afternoon, the place was back to near normal. Horst and Frieda snored in the bedroom.

It was Sunday, and I was way late for my standing date with Martina at her house. Physical and mental exhaustion had dampened my mood for sex, but I still wanted to see her and tell her what had happened.

As soon as I stepped outside the apartment building, two strong hands gripped my upper arm.

"Let's go for a ride, Timo," said a bald young man dressed in a work shirt with rolled up sleeves.

He ushered me into the front seat of a car parked at the curb.

"It's good to see you again, Timo," said Christian's brother with a fake smile. He sat in the driver's seat of the Volga M21, the most expensive Russian made car in 1961. I sat next to him, having been shoved into the black sedan, and my bald, beefy escort sat in the back.

"What's going on?" I asked, then I turned toward the backseat, "What did you do to my sister?"

The hefty, bald guy just looked out the window and smirked.

"Relax, Timo," Christian's brother said as he reached over and massaged my shoulder. Unlike the guy sitting in the backseat who looked like a hard-drinking factory worker, he looked as he did the first time that I had met him—cool, calm, and dressed in a pressed brown suit. "You're in no danger. Yes, we heard about the terrible way someone treated your sister. Despicable and barbaric, but most of all so totally unnecessary.

"Now, let's see. This is Sunday again. Yes, you have a … what's that French word? *Rendezvous* with that little girlfriend of yours. What's her name, Timo?"

I didn't answer, and the backseat guy snickered.

"Ah, yes, I remember now. Martina. Lovely young lady. What a terrible shame if something like what happened to your sister happened to such a beautiful young flower—"

"What do you want!"

During the entire conversation, he had been caressing my shoulder. Now, he gripped it as if I were a child he wanted to keep still.

"Just some information."

"About what?"

"About anything or anyone you know that is associated with anti-Soviet state actions of treason. That's all."

My eyes began to well, but I forced back tears. Tears meant weakness. My dilemma left me weak. Through no fault or wish of my own, I knew of four people who fit into the category he had described. Max and Hannah planned to defect the following week, but I would never betray them. Then there were the workers that Horst had talked about.

"Look, I don't know if it's true. They don't know if it's true or not, but I heard my brother-in-law mention some names."

Shuffling in the backseat told me my brawny escort prepared to take some notes.

"And what were those names?" asked Christian's brother.

I think he said their names were Kurt and Erma or Erna or something like that. That's all I know. I swear it."

His grip on my shoulder loosened. He tapped it as if complimenting a child for a good deed and said, "And now ... you can go. Enjoy yourself. Do whatever your young *schvantz* tells you to do with Martina."

I wanted to punch his fat face and kill the guy in the backseat, but I recognized my helpless situation.

The door slammed behind me, and they drove off laughing.

Tuesday morning, I left the apartment for work.

My encounter with the Stasi had shaken me, but with each passing hour since, I became less and less concerned. When I had reached Martina's house late that Sunday afternoon, she could tell something was wrong. I decided not to involve her, so I told her my sister and brother-in-law had upset me again with their usual badgering about my future. Martina's seductive nature made me forget my problems, and we relished another blissful Sunday of sex. The next day, Horst and Frieda reported that Kurt and Erna did not come to work that day.

I followed my routine of picking up the morning newspaper and reading the headlines before tossing it inside the apartment. A story on the second page read:

Couple Found Drowned

The bodies of Kurt and Erna Schmitt were found in Kindel Lake. Police theorize that the couple had decided to miss work Monday morning and go for a swim. They apparently drowned ...

The Stasi had lied. They *were* barbarians, and I was responsible for the barbaric deaths of two people. I was a snitch, an unwilling member of the National People's Army. The thought made me dizzy, so I sat in the hall and tried not to scream or cry, but the guilt inside me was too strong. I ran into the stairwell and vomited.

Another thought struck me. Max and Hannah were defecting the following week. I was part of the escape plan. Christian's brother would never believe that I knew nothing about my boss's escape.

What should I do?

"Nothing," I said to myself in a hushed voice that echoed in the staircase. There was nothing I could do but live with the guilt.

I went back to the apartment, threw the newspaper inside the door, shut it in a manner not to awaken Horst and Frieda, and went to work.

Chapter 8

Saturday, August 12, 1961

Sven cleared off the coffee table in the Thomas' living room. He took off his shoes, mounted it, and addressed the card players, "Attention, everyone."

It was almost midnight, and the last round of 66 had been played. I never quite understood the game, but it was a popular German pastime among adults. The objective is to score 66 or more points capturing cards in tricks and winning the last trick. This group played a four-handed version—two teams of paired partners sat at each table. Since ten people made up this club, four teams played at the two tables, and the odd team served drinks and snacks until a round had been played. The serving couple rotated with the losing team, who then became the servers through the next round.

The club met on the second Saturday of each month at the Thomas house because of its central location and spacious living/dining room. The other members took turns supplying the refreshments. Max and Hannah always provided coffee, but on a rotating basis, club members supplied the midnight dessert after the games. This night Sven and Dora, his girlfriend for the past thirty years, had brought dessert which they kept hidden in a box.

"Get off that coffee table before you break it or your neck, you idiot!" Dora said from the kitchen.

Sven and Dora had met decades earlier in Hamburg where she made a living as an exotic dancer. Only Sven, with his quick wit and charm, could have lured her away from her lucrative profession. The couple never married but had lived together for decades. Dora fought old age. Her long, reddish brown dyed hair and curvy figure still made her seductive, despite her weathered olive skin. She always dressed like a woman half her age—skirt above the knees and a blouse or dress with a low neckline.

The others laughed at Sven and Dora's standard sparring, and, with her arms folded and her head shaking, Dora strolled into the dining room the same confident way she had promenaded down the runway at a strip club—shoulders back and hips swaying.

Sven lowered his head, smiled, and, as usual, accepted her playful insult.

"Anyway, we have a special dessert and an announcement to make," he said, and stepped down from the table.

Like obedient school children, the members retired to the dining area. The men carried some folding chairs from the card tables for the extra seating needs.

Tradition dictated that the homeowners sat at either end of the long table.

Alex Mauer, a retired building contractor, sat on Max's left. Like Wenzel Vogel seated across from him, Alex was unmarried. Short and rounded, his wardrobe had remained consistent since his retirement a decade earlier. He wore tired, baggy suits that clashed with wide loud-colored ties, white socks, and brown shoes. His perpetual, introspective frown gave the suggestion that he was always thinking or planning.

He grunted and turned away from the sight of Dora's suggestive walk.

The others nicknamed Wenzel "The Mouse" because of his timid and quiet nature. He had worked as a timekeeper in a metal plating and heat-treating factory before it closed after the war. Unlike the others his age, his thinning hair was dark brown. Some suspected him of coloring it which he denied like an innocent child accused of lying. He stood as tall as Max, but his skinny body and nervous disposition made him appear shorter. He, too, wore a suit every day of his retirement, but his outfits, although cheap, fit him with immaculate precision. Standing next to Alex and sketched in caricature, the two resembled Laurel and Hardy.

Wenzel, as he often did, stared at Alex for direction when Sven asked from the kitchen, "Who wants coffee?"

The Lehrs, Gerhard and Magda, sat opposite each other. Gerhard had enjoyed fame as a respected literature professor at Humboldt University in Berlin before the city split in 1949. His dissident opinions about Soviet education forced him to choose retirement over a transfer to an East German labor camp. He sported his typical attire: brown loafers, casual khaki slacks, and a pullover sweater with the collar of a buttoned-down sport shirt sticking out the V-neck. His white hair grew over his ears and the back of his neck, longer than most German men his age, and liver spots dotted his drawn face. One might expect Gerhard to convey the relaxed, thoughtful demeanor of a retired scholar, but he expressed a dour, sad look as he held his wife's hand under the table.

Magda sighed as she listened to gossip exchanged between Hannah and Wenzel. She ran a daycare center in town. Seated next to Wenzel, the two could have passed for brother and sister, maybe even twins. Magda's shiny, dyed-brown hair matched Wenzel's. Even her long, dark skirt and matching jacket resembled Wenzel's suit. Her handsome, charming face contrasted with Wenzel, but they shared the same nervous habits: twiddling thumbs and quick, darting movements in reaction to any sudden noise.

Opposite them sat Ralf, "The Gentle Giant," and Helga Seiler. Ralf was huge and brawny, but as easygoing and passive as he was strong. He sometimes had helped us with heavy hauling jobs. His massive arms hung from his broad, bulging shoulders like heavy canvas sacks filled with coins. Time may have produced the swell beneath his gladiator-like chest, but no one could describe him as fat. He kept his grey hair closely cropped and his face fixed with a smile that seemed to say, "Everything will be fine." The tallest man in the group, he wore loose fitting short-sleeved shirts and dark workpants. He seemed uncomfortable in his own body. Maybe his mammoth exterior made him feel freakish.

"What's taking you two so long in there?" said Max to Sven and Dora, who had been preparing the dessert and coffee in the kitchen.

Sven answered with loud mocking sexual noises followed by, "Just joking. No, seriously I had to find a wheel barrel to load Helga's dessert portion."

"You better find a large, wide wooden spoon, too, so I can stick it up your ass when you come out here," said Helga.

Helga, Ralf's obese wife, couldn't have been more opposite from her husband. Her corpulence and robust character often became the target of Sven's humor. She carried her huge body with confidence and defiance and would fling her once blond, (now ashen) long braided hair behind her. She reminded me of one of those Oktoberfest waitresses, who carry six mugs, each filled with a liter of beer, in each hand, which Helga could still do in her mid-seventies. She even wore dirndl dresses (Bavarian style circular dresses worn with white low-cut tops and aprons at Oktoberfest) as her everyday wear.

The laughter subsided with the dimming overhead light. Sven and Dora carried a huge cake with white icing, red trim, and lettering and set it in front of Hannah. The members "oohed" and "aahed" but expressed confusion at the occasion.

"Our good friend, Max, has an announcement to make," said Sven.

Max stood and addressed everyone, "I did not know that my sneaky friends, Sven and Dora, had made such a fuss with the cake, but Hannah and I wanted to take this occasion to say good-bye to all of you, our best and longtime friends. We are crossing the border into Frohnau on Monday and not coming back."

"*Mein Gott,*" said Magda and Helga, and they rushed to hug Hannah.

Above the din of questions and congratulations, Hannah shouted and sobbed, "I will miss all of you terribly, but I just can't live without my daughter and grandson anymore."

Sven took his elevated position on the coffee table again and announced, "Now, I don't have to tell you that this news stays here and does not leave."

"You just did, you skinny idiot," said Helga. "Of course, we won't say anything."

Dora brought in a tray of plates, cups, and utensils. "Sven, get down from there and get the coffee pot. Hannah, please honor us and cut the first piece," she said and handed her a long, sharp kitchen knife.

Hannah held the knife with two hands. Her eyes welled and saddened as she scanned the faces. Her thoughts must have shifted to her daughter and baby grandson because her melancholy expression brightened into a smile.

The red lettering on the cake read, *All Your Dreams Have Come True*.

"This is both the happiest and saddest day of my life," she said and sliced the first wedge. Her cut had eliminated the word *Dreams* from the red sugary statement.

Chapter 9

Sunday, August 13, 1961, 5:35 a.m.

A piercing scream, like that of a tortured animal awakened Max. He would have been up within the next half hour anyway, but the unnerving shriek had a familiar tone that jarred him. He stepped into his bedside slippers, put on his terrycloth robe hanging on the bathroom door, walked to the back door, and gazed through the screen.

Hannah stood just beyond the chicken coop. The pail of seeds she carried each dawn to feed the chickens and fill with fresh eggs lay on its side next to her, seeds spread on the grass from the impact with the ground.

Max approached Hannah, but she didn't seem to notice. She stood frozen with terror. When he reached her, standing behind the chicken coop, he saw it—a line of border guards spaced half a block apart stood along the East Berlin boundary, north and south as far as one could see. Behind them, workers had removed the rolling barbed wire barrier. In its place they had constructed parallel barbed wire fences about twenty meters apart. Halfway between the laborers sinking timber fence posts and stretching barbed wire, others carried six-meter I-beams from piles. They dropped them into pre-dug holes, so the beams stood upright about three meters above ground, and then poured cement into each hole.

Max recognized the I-beams, the same girders he and I had delivered to Brandenburg weeks earlier. He moved toward a fence worker, but a guard yelled, "Stop!" and ran toward him.

"What's going on?" Max asked as the guard drew near him.

"The workers are not allowed to speak to you. I will answer your questions."

The guard stood as tall as Max but seemed to be faceless. The sun rising from the east hit the brim of his military cap and shaded all his features.

"Okay, what is going on?"

"You are in what is now called 'the exclusion zone.' It's forbidden."

"It's my property."

"Not anymore, sir. All property three meters along the East Berlin and East German borders now belongs to the state."

"I was just going to ask the worker what they were doing."

The guard turned to look at the construction behind him. Maybe he was trying to remember what he was ordered to say when asked. He turned and faced Max.

"They are building a wall."

"A wall? But why?"

"To help us enforce the new restriction. There is to be no more travel of East German citizens to West Berlin."

"What do you mean by 'no more'? What about *Gastarbeiter?*"

Gastarbeiter literally meant, "foreign worker." When Germans used the word back then, they referred to a law that allowed some East German residents to work in West Berlin. That same law permitted us to cross the border and do state sanctioned hauling jobs. It would have also provided the means for Max and Hannah's escape the following day.

"No more."

"What about families? Many of us have family on the other side."

A short silence followed.

"I'm sorry."

A longer silence hung between them as all this sunk into Max's consciousness. Just as the guard turned to return to his post, Max said, "Wait, please. I just have one more question."

The guard stopped but didn't turn toward Max. It was as if he had anticipated the final logical question.

"Why a wall? You can still make arrests for defection."

"There will be no more arrests. This area between the exclusion zone and the wall will be known as 'the death zone.' Our new orders regarding defectors are *shoot to kill*," the guard said with his head down as if ashamed and sauntered back to his post.

"Shoot to kill? That's barbaric," said Max so only he and Hannah could hear.

But Hannah no longer stood beside him. At some point, she had ambled down the exclusion zone toward the other guard. When she was far enough away from Max or the guards to stop her, she bolted across the work area toward Frohnau.

"Do your job!" yelled the faraway guard to the closer border sentinel.

The young border guard froze. It was as if he thought he had misheard his ranking officer's order.

"Do your job," repeated the guard.

Christian raised his rifle, aimed, and squeezed off several repetitive rounds. His pale body shook as he lowered his weapon.

PART II:
THE TUNNEL

Chapter 10

Christmas Eve, 1961, 11:30 p.m.

Max sat alone in front of his fireplace. He drank from a mug of *Glüh-wein*, a warmed dark red traditional German wine enjoyed around Christmas time, and gazed at the photo of Hannah on the mantel above the hearth. The glowing red logs spit orange sparks up the chimney and flashed glimpses of Max's melancholy expression in the dark room.

His eyes had aged with every passing week since Hannah's horrific death. It was the aging of his eyes that made me realize the secret of his youthful appearance. Many hard-working German men of his years looked and acted like him, but it was his eyes that had a look of wonder, curiosity, and joy that children possess when they discover their world each day.

It faded more and more like a burning log from radiance to grey ash.

Sven and I kept the business going, and whenever he felt up to it, Max worked with us. But he was just a man going through the motions. Not even Sven's clowning moved him beyond a forced smile.

Max and Hannah had embraced the holiday season with all the German traditions: a tree lit with candles, the Christmas Market visits, gift exchanging, and parties.

Many thought the Soviet takeover of East Germany in 1949 meant the end of Christian holidays, but Soviet leaders were much too smart to squelch such a beloved and deep-rooted holiday as Christmas within German culture. Instead, they promoted the holiday, but with the subtlety of a sharp sickle, extracted the birth of Christ from it. The week-long Christmas Market where citizens enjoyed food, drink, gifts, and rides for children became a celebration of economic growth and the rise of socialism. The Red Star of Russia rose on Christmas Eve over East Berlin and replaced the symbolic Shining Star of David. In place of Christmas carols, the state published songs and poems such as Erich Weinhart's "The New Star":

> *Above the courtyard, in the icy night*
> *An awakened star is shining bright.*
> *It stands over the window of the poor*
> *With blood red brilliance;*
> *And its five points stream wide and far*
> *In misery, hunger and darkness.*
> *It shines everywhere on earth.*
> *Where poor children are given birth.*
> *Not just one Savior among us stands.*
> *But millions of Saviors in all the lands.*

The Soviets emphasized the Christmas theme of peace but had adapted it for their own purpose. Commercial references to "Peace Christmas" alluded to the motto, "Peace—that is Socialism."

Max put on his lined trench coat that his wife had given him as a Christmas present the previous year. She often teased him about his less than dressy wardrobe. Maybe, he thought, a walk outside in the crisp winter air would cheer him or kindle some holiday spirit. He strolled by the church where he and Hannah would have attended midnight Christmas Eve service. Some light shined through the stained-glass window. Few people attended church services anymore. Mostly elderly women made up the sparse congregations. Soviet philosophy associated religion with weakness and femininity, but that didn't discourage Max from going to church on Sunday. "Only weak men need to flaunt their manhood," he'd say.

He peered into windows and watched families opening gifts, drinking, and laughing in the soft candlelight that illuminated Christmas trees. The most recent popular tree ornament was a small replica of *Sputnik*, the first artificial earth satellite launched into space—a Russian achievement. He wondered how many children growing up in this socialist-defined holiday would ever know the true origins of Christmas.

A strange ritual stopped him as he approached the Becker household just a few houses from his own. Several people dressed in black stood in the front yard. They looked as if they were scanning the neighborhood to see if anyone watched them.

Max hid beneath some bushes and watched.

One of them nodded, and they split up. A hooded figure headed Max's way, so he crunched closer to the ground and beneath some foliage. The person looked both ways down the block, emptied a bucket of something onto the bushes, and hurried back to the house. The substance trickled through the branches and landed on Max's head.

Max waited until all the dark figures returned to the house before he emerged from beneath the hedges and grabbed a fistful of the substance from his hair.

"What the hell?" he whispered to himself.

It was only black dirt.

Curiosity led him across the Beckers' lawn, and he cracked open the unlocked door. The house was dark except for light coming from a stairwell leading to the cellar. He crept like a burglar toward the cellar doorway and peeked down the stairs. The men who had emptied the dirt pails were digging a tunnel beneath the dim light of a single hanging light bulb.

"I'm afraid your old curious eyes have led you to your death, Max Thomas."

Max felt the cold double barrels of a shotgun against the back of his neck.

"Turn slowly, old man, and come with me into the kitchen," said Erwin Becker, who backed up into the hallway and motioned with the shotgun for Max to sit at the kitchen table as he switched on the overhead light.

Max pivoted in slow motion and looked up at Erwin, the eldest of the five Becker brothers. He worked in East Berlin as a chauffeur for the East German Parliament, but one look at him made you realize he was hired more for his muscular, bodyguard physique than his driving skills. His brothers worked as laborers at an ice factory in East Berlin. Erwin reminded Max of a younger version of his card playing friend, Ralf—tall, massive body, flat stomach, short cropped brown hair. The main difference between Erwin and Max's easygoing friend was in the face. Ralf displayed a distinctive, kind, gentle expression. Erwin exhibited a characteristic scowl as he forced Max into the kitchen.

"Sit and keep your hands where I can see them."

Max sat in a chair across the table from Erwin and tapped his memory of the Becker boys growing up. Their father, a low-ranking Nazi officer, had ruled his household like Hitler commanded the nation, with military preciseness. He had disciplined his boys and wife using swift, powerful kicks punctuated with the stiff point of his brown boot. He died at the hands of Russian soldiers not far from the bunker where Hitler committed suicide. His widow raised the boys, but her weak body and passive nature allowed them to run wild. Although none of them had ever spent time in prison, their reputation in Glienicke/Nordbahn included petty theft, arson, assault, and suspicion in the disappearance of a teen-aged girl in the mid-1950s.

"So, what's the reason for the gun and the threat? I saw nothing. You're doing some repairs or improvements in your cellar. Big deal," said Max.

Erwin sat back in his chair, kept his shotgun barrels resting on the table but pointing at Max's chest, and said, "Oh, Max Thomas, we've known each other a long time. You may be old, but you're not stupid. If you haven't guessed that we're building an escape tunnel under the wall, you would have, eventually. Then you'd leak it to your card club friends. Sorry, Max Thomas, but it must be this way. After all, with your wife gone now, it would be a long time before anyone would miss your old, tired body buried somewhere away from your abandoned property."

Max stared at the gun barrels and wondered why Erwin used both his first and last name. As obedient youngsters they had addressed him as *Herr* Thomas. When they became unruly kids, he became Old Man Thomas. They, as adults, simply called him Max and treated him with measured respect. It occurred to him that using his first and last name put some distance between him and Erwin. Obituaries referred to the dead with both names. Erwin was preparing himself to be a killer, and yet Max felt unafraid, even calm. Since Hannah's death, maybe he had primed himself to die. Maybe he even wished it. Still, he couldn't resist the opportunity to outfox his younger adversary.

"Since I'm going to die anyway, tell me, how long do you think it will take to finish this tunnel?"

"Well, with all of us working at our day jobs, we can only dig and get rid of the dirt for several hours at night and on Sunday. We figure we can finish before March and be gone before spring."

Max smiled, put his hands behind his head, stared at the ceiling light, and said, "Erwin, Erwin, Erwin, I always took you as the smartest of your brothers. You should know that every day it takes you to build this tunnel you risk being discovered. A border guard or the National People's Army now circle by here every fifteen minutes or so. Between guards and nosey neighbors turning you in, or one of your disguised-in-black brothers getting caught dumping dirt around the neighborhood, you're bound to get caught."

"We'll take those risks."

"I could have you out before February, but then that's impossible for a dead man."

After a long silence, Erwin said, "Keep talking, Max."

Max noted the change of address to just his first name.

"Instead of your brothers sneaking all over town dumping dirt like a gang of amateur burglars, you could just dump it into one of my trucks parked nearby. During the day, my workers could haul it away and disperse it just like another typical job. Also, some of my more able retired 'card club friends' as you call them could dig during the day while you and your brothers work your day jobs."

Erwin continued his wide-eyed gaze and silence before asking, "How do I know you're not bluffing, and how do I know you or one of your friends wouldn't turn us in?"

"You don't, but it's much less of a risk than the one you're taking now. Think about it, Erwin. You have two assurances on your side. First, we'd expect to be paid, and second, everyone knows the reputation of the Becker boys. The expectation of a reward and the fear of revenge from you and your brothers, I promise you, are more than enough to insure absolute secrecy."

"How much would you expect to get paid?"

"Nothing, just a place in your tunnel."

This time the silence lasted almost five long minutes.

"Simon!" Erwin called out as if summoning a dog.

Simon, the youngest and somewhat feeble-minded brother, appeared in the kitchen. He gasped and held his mouth wide open when he saw his brother holding Max hostage.

"Here, hold this," Erwin said, handed him the shotgun, and gave him his seat. "Blow him to bits if he tries anything."

Simon obeyed him, and Erwin retreated to the basement. The young man tried to put on a menacing expression, but his trembling body and unblinking teacup-sized eyes made him look like a terrified little boy. The youngest and weakest brother sat speechless with his signature half-opened mouth twitching. His stringy, sandy hair matted with dirt and his black sweatshirt soaked in sweat, he clutched the gun stock as if letting it go might be fatal.

Max, fearing any slight movement might trigger Simon's anxiety or literal interpretation of his brother's instruction, kept still.

The clanging of pickaxing and shoveling ceased as Erwin spoke to his brothers. His exact words were inaudible, but following his speech, loud arguing and an occasional "*Nein, Nein*" resonated up the stairwell and into the kitchen.

After what seemed like a week to Max, all four brothers emerged from the cellar and stood in the kitchen.

"We've come to a conclusion."

Simon lifted the butt of the shotgun and aimed the barrels at Max's heart.

Chapter 11

Christmas Day, 1961, noon

Frieda and Horst prepared to leave for the day. Every Christmas, Horst's parents who lived in Hoppegarten, about forty kilometers and as many minutes away, invited them along with Horst's two sisters for dinner. I was not on the guest list—just as well. The attempt at a warm family gathering was genuine. They exchanged gifts and ate a Christmas goose dinner with potato salad, just like a normal, civilized German family. Then Horst's father brought out the liquor, the beginning of the end. As the alcohol took hold, accusations of family favoritism, immorality, theft, and almost everything excluding the only provable allegation, drunkenness, grew louder and louder.

Martina's parents had caved to her insistence that I share in their Christmas dinner. They disliked me as a possible mate for their daughter. I often thought that Olaf's persistence that I become a border guard and Martina's assertion that I better myself came from them.

When I knocked on her door, Martina answered, joined me outside, and closed the door.

"Something wrong?" I asked.

"No," she said with a girlish laugh and cocked her head to the side, "I just thought it best if we exchanged gifts in private. Here, open yours first."

She handed me a small box wrapped in red paper with a green bow. My hands trembled from the cold as I ripped off the paper and opened the hinged lid of the black box. It was a silver plated Ruhla pocket watch.

"It's beautiful," I said.

"I wanted to get you a wristwatch, but you said you didn't like them because they would get damaged or caught on things when you worked."

"But it must have cost a fortune."

"No, not really. Olaf bought it at a military discount. It's the same watch issued to the border patrol."

I tried not to frown. Yes, it was a beautiful and thoughtful gift, but the subtle message from her and her brother was clear—join the East German border guards.

"Now open yours," I said and pulled a similar sized unwrapped box with a single silver bow from my coat pocket.

Martina grabbed the box and removed the top, careful to keep the bow intact. Her eyes widened, and her mouth opened in a gasp. She lifted the delicate gold chain and held the ruby birthstone pendant, so it sparkled in the sunlight.

"How did you know?"

"I saw your eyes glitter just like that jewel when you saw Nadine wearing one just like it at that party last summer."

"Help me put it on," she said.

I fumbled with the clasp. She held her hair up and scolded me for my clumsiness. As soon as it was attached, she turned and kissed me with her arms wrapped around my neck.

A knock on the window from inside and Olaf's words, "Get in here, you lovers, before I have to use my military weapons to separate you," interrupted our embrace.

I stamped the light snow from my feet before entering and issued a general "Merry Christmas" to all.

They returned the greeting with mixed enthusiasm.

Olaf, red-faced and inebriated, rushed towards me with a warm cup of *Glühwein* and said, "Drink up, Timo."

He wore his dress guard uniform. Since he had become a border guard, he seemed to dress only in his military issued clothes.

"Olaf, isn't it hard to sleep with your guard hat and brown boots on?"

"No, I don't sleep in my uniform," he said with sincerity, unable to detect my sarcasm.

Martina joined her mother in the kitchen, so I was left in the living room with Olaf, his father settled in his cushy, cloth recliner chair, and a strange-looking elderly woman seated across from him.

"Sit down, Timo," said the father and motioned for Olaf to bring another chair from the dining room.

"Thank you, Herr Schmidt."

I liked him despite his indifference toward me. If I were Martina's father, I would have wanted the best for her, also. He had sandy greyish hair, a handsome but weathered face, and a strong, stocky build. On this day, he wore a bright red flannel shirt, brown corduroy pants, white socks, and shiny brown fur slippers, an obvious Christmas gift.

The old woman sitting in the rocking chair across from him stared at me as if I were a leper. Her long black dress, a white lace handkerchief in her lap, and the dour, dead expression on her face reminded me of a painting, *Whistler's Mother*, in an art book issued to us in primary school.

"This is Timo, Tante Eva. He is Martina's boyfriend," Herr Schmidt said in a loud voice.

"*Hallo!*" she said.

Herr Schmidt, before repeating his words in a louder voice, said to me, "She is my ninety-two-year-old aunt from Brandenburg."

After his second introduction, she asked, louder than anyone had spoken thus far, "What do you do, boy?"

Olaf answered, "He's a hauler, Tante Eva."

She looked at Olaf as if he were a talking dog and said, "What the hell is that?"

"Time for dinner," said Martina's mother from the kitchen doorway.

Frau Schmidt cooked like a chef, but the key to her hearty meals was her hearty self. It was difficult not to like her. In her early forties, she was neither heavy nor thin, neither plain nor beautiful. Her short brown hair, always combed and clean, stayed in place as she shuffled around the kitchen in her lace-sleeved apron over a red and green Christmas dress with long sleeves. Her grinning face expressed some level of joy in everything she did.

She had prepared a feast of *Maultaschensuppe* (stuffed dumpling soup), smoked-ham rolls, roast pork with sauerkraut, sausages, a small roast duck, chestnut stuffing, spinach, potato salad, Riesling wine, and spiced wine.

Before eating, we held hands and Herr Schmidt said a prayer of thanks. Neither Olaf nor Martina bowed their heads.

Halfway through the meal she blurted, "*Hallo*! What the hell does a hauler do?"

Again, Olaf answered, "He hauls building materials, farm products, and sometimes garbage, Tante Eva."

I wanted to hit him, but I was glad that he had answered for me. She made me feel awkward enough without having to scream across the table.

"How do you expect to support my niece doing that?"

Martina put a cloth napkin over her mouth to cover her laugh.

A long pause signaled I would have to answer this one, but Olaf broke the silence.

"He won't have to. I'm trying to convince him to become a border guard like me."

"Who the hell asked you?" she said.

This time I covered my face with a napkin and felt compelled to lighten the dialogue.

"So, Tante Eva, I understand Herr and Frau Schmidt visit you every Sunday. That must be nice."

"They want my money when I'm dead."

Martina laughed out loud.

"Stop it, Martina," her mother scolded.

Herr Schmidt said, "Tante Eva, you know that's not—"

"*Hallo!* Anything for dessert?"

"Of course, Tante Eva, I'll get it," said Frau Schmidt and escaped to the kitchen.

The coffee with butter cookies and, later, Black Forest cake wasn't enough to counter our fatigue after that meal. We retired to the living room where Tante Eva fell into a deep sleep in the rocker. Frau Schmidt covered her with a shawl.

"Thank God she's out," said Herr Schmidt.

Olaf got up and turned on the television set. The government detested that TV stations from West Germany could be viewed by East Germans. They tried various methods to keep us from watching these "corruptive" shows. They jammed the airwaves and even encouraged us teens to damage any TV antennas we spotted pointing west. When nothing else worked, the government produced *Der Schwarze Kanal* (The Black Channel) in 1961. It consisted of western broadcasts re-edited with Communist commentary by host Karl-Eduard von Schnitzler. Olaf wanted to watch this, but his parents trumped his choice with a Christmas concert on another channel.

A knock on the door interrupted our television viewing. Martina answered it.

The guest's entrance signaled my departure.

I thanked my host and hostess, grabbed my coat, and headed for the door.

"Merry Christmas, Timo," Christian said with a warm smile, as I brushed past him and opened the door.

I looked back at him but couldn't speak. My stare was as chilling as the cold air rushing inside. I didn't want to hate him, but I did.

Martina followed me outside, closed the door, and clasped her arms against the cold.

"That was terribly rude, Timo."

"Rude? As rude as shooting the wife of a good man, my friend and boss? Killing a wonderful woman whose only sin was loving her family too much?"

She looked away and said, more to herself than to me, "You know he was only doing his job."

I took a step towards her and said, "Yes, his job, so much nobler than that of a hauler."

I turned and sprinted away toward my destination. It was getting dark. With every step through the woods I felt more alone. By the time I had reached Max's house, Christmas night, 1961, had turned pitch black. Of course, my loneliness didn't compare to Max's, but somehow, I figured two lonely men might salvage Christmas with a couple mugs of warm *Glühwein*.

As soon as Max opened the door, I noticed that his youthful eyes had returned.

"Come in, Timo. I'm glad you're here. Sit down while I get you some *Glühwein* I've kept simmering on the stove."

My first inclination was that he was drunk, but he wasn't. I sat at the dining room table, well-lit from the overhead fixture and cluttered with sketches and plans.

"So, it looks like you've been working on something important here," I said as he set the warm mug of wine in front of me and another for himself.

"Timo, Timo, something miraculous happened last night, and you are a part of it whether you want to be or not."

He filled me in on his Christmas Eve walk and his discovery of the Becker tunnel.

"All five Becker brothers hovered over me in their kitchen. Simon raised the gun and aimed it at my chest. I perspired through my shirt as his finger quivered on the trigger just as Erwin said, 'Simon, give me that gun. Max Thomas is our friend.' During the time they argued my fate in the cellar, I thought I didn't want to live any more, but at that moment, I felt like Hannah was watching over me. I can still see her dazed expression while she watched them build that wall—that wall separating her from her daughter and grandson. That wall that led her to her death. She wanted me to have the freedom denied to her … my Hannah."

The mention of Hannah's name signaled a moment of silence.

"Max, you said this involved me whether I liked it or not. What did you mean?"

I tried to sip my *Glühwein*, that steaming blood-red wine, but it nearly burnt my lips, so I set it on the table to cool.

"You're a part of this in at least three ways. First, you know about it, so your silence is important, not just for my sake and the freedom of the others, but your own."

He must have read my confused expression.

"Yes, Timo, for your own sake." He took a sip of his wine and seemed to be filtering his thoughts. "The Becker brothers are not choir boys. They would just as easily kill and bury you with a shovel, as hand you one to help them dig their tunnel. That brings me to the second way that you're involved. You work for me, and from now on we have two jobs—whatever work we normally must do, plus working on the Becker tunnel."

"How will we be working on it?"

"That's what I've been planning since last night."

He sat in the chair closest to me and shifted all his paperwork between us. His plans included a daily work schedule focused on a weekly goal. He, Sven, and I would work the mornings filling our regular hauling contracts. During that time, his card playing friends would dig or build wooden forms, in the Becker cellar.

"The three of us will break for lunch near Kindel Lake. After eating, we'll load some flat rocks from the shore and return. We'll unload the rocks in front of the Beckers' house. We and the Beckers will explain to anyone who asks that they're building a decorative stone wall in their front yard. Between unloading rocks and border guard patrols, we'll empty buckets of dirt into our covered truck. The next day, during our regular hauling routes, we'll disperse the dirt."

I took a sip of my warm *Glühwein* and weighed my next questions. "Max, I know these people are your close friends, but have you talked to them about this? This is a risky venture. Once you mention it, they are involved, just like me. They may not want to be a part of it. Most importantly," I hesitated, "Can you trust them not to tell?"

He closed his eyes, grinned, and nodded.

"Timo, don't think I haven't thought of all these matters. No, except for you and Sven, I haven't revealed this to anyone. He and Dora visited today to celebrate Christmas. While Dora made coffee, I shared my idea with Sven. He pledged their support. The others? I don't know. That is, I don't know if they want to help, but I'm not worried about their confidence. I've known these people for sixty or more years, Timo. Our trustworthiness has been tested many times over things far more important and far less trivial.

"We haven't met to play 66 since Hannah's death. I'm inviting them to come play before the New Year, and I'll share all this with them at that time. They'll all come because they've been hounding me to socialize more since her death. But I'll be asking for one more level of involvement, the third way is for you, too. In exchange for our help, the Beckers have allowed me ten places in line to escape to the West. Hannah is gone. I'm offering that place to you."

The last of my wine tasted cold, and my answer surprised even me. "I don't think I can go, Max."

Max, expressionless, sat back and said, "I thought you might be hesitant. What is it? Your family? Your girlfriend?"

"Not my family, or what's left of it, that's for sure. I guess it is my girlfriend, Martina, although I don't even know if she's still my girlfriend."

"Something happened?"

"I was with her family for Christmas dinner, and—," I stopped myself from bringing up Christian which would remind him of Hannah's death and just said, "We just had a minor fight."

He nodded and said, "Well, I'm making the decision even tougher for you. If you stay, my business, this house, everything is yours. I'm leaving it to you."

My empty mug fell from my hands and bounced on the thick rug. Since I was a little boy following Max and riding in his truck, I dreamed of running his business. I would be my own boss ... except for the Soviet government, and I would no longer have to live in that cramped apartment with drunks.

"Are you sure you want to do this, Max? I don't just mean giving this all to me. I mean leaving and going to the West. What will you do there? How will you live? What about the others? Will they want to leave, too?"

He retrieved my cup and set it in front of me.

"The others? I can't speak for them. I'll find out at our card night. As for me, I know I can stay with my stepdaughter, her husband, and child. They have discreetly made the offer through letters. We must be careful. The government screens all communication with the West. Somehow, I feel that I owe the risk to Hannah. Anyway, they would be getting a live-in babysitter.

"And as for leaving everything to you," he put his big heavy hand on my shoulder, "you're the only family I have here now."

We sat in silence for a minute. Max seemed to be far away in thought.

"What is it, Max?"

"There's something I didn't mention. While I sat upstairs with that half-wit Simon pointing a gun at me, I could barely hear the other brothers arguing downstairs. From what I could gather, the major objection came from three of the four brothers. They made a good argument against letting us escape with them. They said some of us might be too old and feeble to crawl through it. We might hinder or even ruin the whole operation. Erwin seemed to pacify them. He spoke for a long time in a hushed voice, so I couldn't hear what he said. I know my offer to cut the time of building the tunnel in more than half was strong, but I have my suspicions. Ah! Maybe I'm just being too skeptical. I guess it's just hard to trust the Becker boys after knowing them so long. I forget that they are men and not just mischievous little boys anymore."

As I listened to Max, the elation of owning his home and business gave way to clearer thinking. What would Martina think? Would she marry me, and would we live together in this house? The idea of living with more freedom in the West appealed to me, also.

"You know, Max, I'm not sure which of your offers is better, living here with your house and business or living there with nothing but my freedom. What do you think I should do?"

Max laughed, took our cups to the kitchen, refilled them, and returned. This time he sat at the head of the table and said, "Timo, you're not a child. You don't have the luxury or the misfortune of adults making decisions for you. That's the price you pay for growing up. Adults carry the burden of making their own choices. I treat you like a man. Regard yourself the same."

"When would you like a definite answer?"

"This is a life decision, Timo. Take all the time you need." He pulled a calendar/planner from the papers and pointed to a square. "If all goes well, the tunnel will be completed on Thursday, January 25th. The Beckers will probably want to leave that night. My offers are good right up until that time.

"Now, if you'll excuse me. I'll be finishing my wine in bed. It's been a long Christmas holiday. When you finish your *Glühwein*, let yourself out or sleep on the couch."

He went upstairs to his room as I sipped my warm beverage and closed my eyes.

The mantel clock struck and awakened me.

I reached into my pocket and retrieved my new watch. It was midnight.

Christmas was over.

Chapter 12

December 26, 1961, 9:10 a.m.

Sven leaned on the iron railing of the narrow balcony outside his and Dora's sixth floor apartment. The building was only a few blocks from where I lived—same type of dingy, colorless complex as ours. He wore only boxer shorts, a thin t-shirt, and a pair of terrycloth slippers, and of course his Irish flat cap as he alternated puffing on his cigarette and sipping from a cup of coffee.

"What the hell are you doing out in the freezing cold in just your underwear?" asked Dora from inside.

He snuffed out his cigarette on the railing, spread his arms, and spoke as if he were addressing a crowd below.

"I'm giving all the women of Glienicke/Nordbahn and East Berlin their Christmas gift, a glimpse of the most beautiful male body in all of Europe."

"Christmas is over. Get your old, skinny *arsch* in here before you catch pneumonia."

He dashed inside, closed the patio door behind him, and gave Dora a bear hug that lifted her off her feet.

"Put me down, you crazy fool, you're cold as ice," she complained.

She poured him another cup of coffee and one for herself. They sat at their kitchen table and ate from a plate of Christmas cookies.

After a short silence, Dora asked, "Are you going to tell me?"

"What?"

"What you and Max talked about last night when I was making coffee?"

Sven flicked the cookie on his plate back and forth with his finger as he contemplated his words.

"He wants to start up the card night again next week."

"*Wunderbar*. It's about time he stopped grieving and started living again."

"There's more to it than that."

Dora put her cup down and gave him a quizzical look.

"He's going to propose a question to all of us. You see, he made a deal with the Becker brothers on Christmas Eve." Sven told her about the tunnel and the agreement he had made in exchange for the brothers allowing the card players to escape with them. "He'll want to know everyone's decision the morning after card night."

"What are you going to tell him?"

"I wanted to hear your thoughts."

Dora looked into her now almost empty cup and thought for several minutes. The dim reflection off the black coffee may have reminded her of her younger self and Sven.

"It's risky," she said, "and we're not young anymore. What are your thoughts?"

"I think we should go," Sven said without hesitation.

"Why?" she asked and lit a cigarette.

"What do we have here?"

"What do we have there?"

"Our dream."

"What dream?" she leaned forward and blew out a puff of smoke. "You mean our dream of running our own tavern? That dream that died when the Soviets converted the government to communism? Sven, we're old. The dream is dead."

"Are we dead!"

"No."

Sven took the cigarette from her mouth, inhaled, and said, "Then neither are our dreams."

She sat back and closed her eyes. She remained that way for several minutes, then opened them, and said, "You're right, Sven. I've always kept the dream, and the dream has kept me alive … and you, too. Call Max right now and tell him we're with him."

"There's no need to call him. I told him 'yes' last night."

Chapter 13

December 29, 1961, 8:30 a.m.

My knuckles stung from knocking on Martina's front door. We hadn't communicated since Christmas Day when I made my "rude" exit. I needed to know if she was still angry with me. We were supposed to attend a *Silvester* party on Sunday. *Silvester* is the German term for New Year's Eve, celebrated with parties and fireworks, much like the rest of the Western World. *She must be home*, I thought. Her parents worked that day, but schools were out from Christmas Eve through New Year's Day.

Max had given me the week off. The hauling business was slow between the holidays. He took this day to prepare for his card club that night.

Just as I pulled my cold, shaking hand from my pocket for a final knocking, it occurred to me that she could be at the library. She worked there after school, but since school wasn't in session, she might be working the full day.

I ran through the woods and reached the steps of The German Central Library Glienicke/Nordbahn Branch at about 8:55. I pulled on the brass doorknob, but it was locked, so I peered through the glass. Martina and the head librarian stood at the front desk sorting books from the return box. Martina ignored me, but the other woman pointed to the clock inside and held up five fingers indicating my waiting time.

My attention turned toward the main street. The bakery, pharmacy, and grocery store had been opened for almost an hour, and a few people walked along the sidewalk. A mangy dog pawed a plastic garbage bag set out by the baker for pick up.

The library doors rattled behind me as Martina unlocked them, but she turned her back when I entered and tried to talk to her. She grabbed a pile of books from the desk where they had been sorted and headed toward the shelves. I snatched a pile and followed her.

The head librarian sneered at me. This woman had never liked me, and the feeling was mutual. My appearance signaled a distraction from her employee's duties, whatever menial jobs librarian assistants do. Tall and slim-figured, she must have only been around thirty but appeared anxious to become old and crotchety. I supposed that someone with a gifted imagination might find her attractive, but I had seen border guards who possessed more personality and feminine appeal.

"Your boss told me to help you file these books," I said in a hushed voice, although no one else was using the library.

"No, she didn't, and I don't need your help."

"Yes, she did. She said you were in an awful snit over something and needed cheering up. Then she said if I didn't come over here right away, she'd jump right over the desk and rape me on the table because she couldn't help herself."

Martina burst into laughter.

"Quiet!" her boss said as if scolding children in church.

"Come on, Martina. I know I was, as you said, 'rude,' but Max is like a father to me and Hannah *was* like my mother."

She was giving in but kept working and said nothing. When we finished shelving the stacks, she said, "We can talk after I finish work at five," and went behind the main counter. The head librarian retreated to her office and closed the door.

I browsed through the card catalogue, took a few notes, and roamed between the bookshelves.

Several people now occupied the reading tables and checked out books. I stood in line behind a little boy and his mother and waited to sign out my findings. I handed her two books, *The Art of Forgiveness* and *Female Psychology*.

"One is for me, and one is for a friend."

She grinned, processed the books and said, "I'll see you Sunday."

I walked home through the woods which appeared all too bright and beautiful for this cold winter's day.

Chapter 14

December 30, 1961

Sven raised his coffee cup and interrupted the chatter at the dining table in Max's house. It was dessert time. The card club had convened that night for the first time since Hannah's death. This left nine players, two tables of four, and one person to serve. Max insisted the others play while he waited on them, but they forced him to sit in on a few games. Overall, everyone appeared cheerful and glad to resume playing 66.

"Friends, I think I speak for all of us," said Sven, "when I say we miss and will always love our dear Hannah."

Silence followed.

"We do, at the same time," he continued, "pledge our love and support to our host, Max Thomas."

Everyone applauded which prompted Max to speak. He stayed seated and fought back tears at the thought of Hannah and the warmth of his friends.

"*Danke*, all of you. I'll always be mournful when I think of Hannah, but something has happened this week which has sweetened her memory and redirected my thoughts."

Max started his story with his Christmas Eve walk and ended with the deal he had made with the Becker brothers.

Wenzel "The Mouse" stood up. Shaking and speaking with a quivering voice, he said, "Shame on you, Max Thomas. Pledging our help without our knowledge, and worse, making a deal with those hoodlum Becker boys. Now that they know we have knowledge of their tunnel, they'll hold us responsible if it is found out and kill us all. You made a deal with the devil!"

"Oh, sit down you mouse," said Gerhard Lehrs. "Max was pleading for his life. If it was you, you would have promised them the world while you shit your pants. You don't have to be a part of it. As for me and Magda, this is the best gift of the season. We've talked about it many times. I hate these fucking Soviets taking us over. I had a great life at Humboldt University. Now, I'm nothing. They have successfully squashed all free thinking and scholarly research here. Most of my colleagues have defected."

"I saw something on West Berlin television about that," said Dora as she shifted from side to side in her chair. "They interviewed these intellectuals who fled to West Berlin, Great Britain, and the United States. The rest of the world calls it 'The Brain Drain' because the best East German minds left for the respect and academic freedom at universities in the West."

"I don't know what they call it. I just know that Gerhard and I want to be part of it," said Magda. She looked at her hands as she spoke and refused to talk directly to the group.

"It's easy for you and Gerhard to decide," said Helga. "You have no family here, and you have something to look forward to on the other side. This decision rips me apart. We have family on both sides and possessions." She buried her head in her arms and cried.

Ralf, her "Gentle Giant" husband, cuddled and comforted her.

Former building contractor, Alex Mauer, put his arm around Max and said, "I for one am with you, Max. One hundred per cent."

Sven and Dora began scolding the dissenters, but Max stopped them.

"That's enough. Everyone who has spoken has a right to his or her opinion."

The silence returned, and Max continued.

"I have placed a heavy burden on all of you, but I judge none of you on what you want to do. This is a huge decision. Sleep on it, but I must know your choice soon. I'm going to bed. Let yourselves out with no more arguing here. Tomorrow morning at nine-thirty I'll go over all the details here at the table. If you're here, fine. If not, that's fine, too. Good night."

He went upstairs and went to bed.

Chapter 15

December 31, 9:00 a.m.

I don't remember seeing Max as nervous as he was that morning. The dining table had all the paperwork he had shown me on Christmas Day, but it was stacked and organized as if he were prepared to give a presentation before a board of directors. He juggled a stack of coffee cups and saucers when I entered through the front door.

"Expecting company again?" I asked. "I thought you had your card club last night."

"I did. Get the coffee pot from the kitchen, and I'll tell you all about it."

I brought the electric coffeemaker from the kitchen counter, set it on the table, and plugged it into the outlet. Max had bought the percolator for Hannah two years earlier because she loved entertaining friends with coffee and pastries.

"How did it go? Did you tell them about the tunnel?"

He flopped into a chair, exhaled as if he had just run a race, and nodded.

"Yes, I told them, but it didn't go as well as I had expected."

"What do you mean?"

"I knew I could count on Alex Mauer because even retired construction contractors are always looking for a building challenge, and we're going to need his engineering mind. Sven and Dora are in, of course. I knew that. The Lehrs surprised me. They're intellectuals. Intellectuals tend to be cautious. I thought they would be against it. As it turns out, being intellectuals makes them eager to get out. They talked about something called 'The Brain Drain' here that's driving all the smart people out of East Germany."

I sat across from him, and we both waited for the red light on the coffeepot to flash.

"Sounds like you have some strong support."

"Not strong enough, Timo." He leaned forward, put his elbows on the table, and shook his head while speaking. "Wenzel Vogel, we call him the Mouse because he's so timid, berated me for even mentioning the Becker tunnel, and maybe he's right. Just knowing about it and not reporting it could put us all in trouble with the government. Reporting it could lead to serious trouble from the Becker brothers. We could surely use Ralf. He's the strongest of all of us, but Helga has family ties here. If she stays, he stays."

The red light signaled that the coffee was ready.

"Max, you've often told me that you can't please everyone."

"Yes, but you don't have to go out of your way to displease them or make their lives miserable. Anyway, we'll find out within the half hour, who, if any, are still with me. I told them to sleep on it, and we'd go over the details this morning at nine-thirty."

We stared at the mantel clock just before the single chime announced quarter past the hour. It also produced a tranquil silence between us.

"Timo," Max said in a soft voice just above the quietness, "have you thought any more about my offers?"

I just looked down at the table top.

"It's okay. I'm not pressing you, but just in case you choose to stay, there are things you should know. I know you can run the business.

You've been watching me and pestering me with questions since you were a little boy, but you know very little about running this house. Follow me."

He led me on a house tour from the upstairs bedrooms to the dirt floor cellar. Over the years, I had been everywhere in his home, but this was the type of tour reserved for new house owners. We explored hidden closets and shelving that stored cleaning supplies, utility controls, and electrical fuses. The expedition included a two-minute demonstration on boiler maintenance in the cellar and the discovery of a safe behind a wall panel upstairs.

"The safe combination is hidden in the chicken coop. Grab your coat, and I'll show you how to tend the chickens. I had to educate myself about that. It used to be Hannah's job."

The snow crunched beneath our boots as we walked to the little wooden barn behind the house. I was overwhelmed. A sixteen-year-old, particularly one who has grown up in apartments, paid no attention to dwelling maintenance. In a teen's mind, the previous generation had built structures for the warmth and comfort of the next generation. When those structures broke down, the older age group either fixed the problem or the structure healed itself.

He showed me how to feed the chickens and to gather eggs. The chickens seemed unfazed by our presence, but as we moved toward them, they hustled out of our path or jumped from their nests on the shelving. Some resisted movement from their nesting until Max moved his hand beneath them. Under one such chicken, he removed the straw, called me toward him, and pointed to the shelf floor.

"This is the combination to the safe. That's the last thing you need to know."

Max had carved three two-digit numbers into the wood. I laughed at his effort to disguise the numbers as a safe combination by drawing a line beneath them and adding up the sum.

"What's so funny?" he asked.

"Nothing. We better go back to the house. Your guests are due to arrive."

We reentered the house through the back door. Voices from the dining room resounded into the kitchen where we stamped our boots on the mat. Max walked to the doorway that led to the dining room. As I shut the door behind us, I won't forget the look on Max's face when he saw who showed up for the Becker tunnel. It was that astonished, almost fearful expression of one who walks into a surprise party held in his honor.

"Did you think I'd let you do this foolish thing without your best man behind you?" asked Wenzel Vogel.

I entered the dining room behind Max. The entire card party group was seated at the table. Helga poured coffee, passed the cups around and said, "And who did you think was going to cook healthy, hearty meals for you old idiots after you worked your pathetic bodies all day digging a tunnel?"

The jovial atmosphere evaporated into silence when they saw me standing next to Max. He put his arm around my shoulders and said, "Don't worry. Timo is with us, at least for the hard work. He'll be the young blood we'll need for our 'old, pathetic bodies' as Helga says. He'll decide later if he wants to crawl through the tunnel with us."

"I just thought of something," said Gerhard. "The average age of the Becker brothers is about thirty-five. The average age of our card club is seventy-five. That's a forty-year difference."

An ominous silence followed. What was his point? That the Beckers' youth was a threat of some kind? Should we be wary of them?

Gerhard rose, put his arm around me, smiled, and said, "But by adding Timo's sixteen years to our average, we're younger than all the Beckers put together."

The cheery ambiance returned.

I acknowledged their warm welcomes and excused myself from the meeting. On Christmas Day, Max had gone over my part and his over-all plan for the others.

Outside, the thin layer of snow intensified the glare of the bright morning sunlight. With every step, my eyes adjusted to the brightness and the life-changing decision confronting me.

Herr Schmidt's cushy chair looked comfortable, but his heavier torso had molded a deep indentation into the seat that forced my elbows too high on the cloth armrests. Still, I pretended to be the man-of-the-house and read the Sunday edition of *Neues Deutschland* with my feet up on the ottoman while Martina did the dinner dishes in the kitchen. We were playing *Haus*, as children called it.

Herr and Frau Schmidt had left that morning, as they did every Sunday, for Tante Eva's house in Brandenburg, but this time they would spend the night and celebrate *Silvester* and New Year's Day with her. They had wanted Martina to join them, but she insisted that she needed to study for final exams scheduled at her EOS (college prep) school in a few days. It was a partial lie. Her university prep school did hold mid-year exams after the holiday break, but Martina never needed to study. Unlike me, who had to review over and over just to ensure a passing grade, Martina's brain stored information like well-organized data and documents in a steel file cabinet.

Continuing my role as man-of-the-house, I read the headline aloud, "1961: THE YEAR IN REVIEW." *Neues Deutschland* embraced that theme for its Sunday, New Year's Day publication. Of course, like most newspapers in East Germany, Soviet propaganda influenced every story. The biggest story in the world was the erection of the Berlin Wall, yet *Neues Deutschland* played it down. The paper focused on the futility of attempted escapes. It reported that over 500 people had died trying to escape East Germany via the Berlin border and reiterated the Soviet position by reprinting The Socialist Unity Party's Agitation Department, Berlin District Manifesto posted in the 1950s:

> *Both from the moral standpoint as well as in terms of the interests of the whole German nation, leaving the GDR is an act of political and moral backwardness and depravity.*
>
> *Those who let themselves be recruited objectively serve West German Reaction and militarism, whether they know it or not. Is it not despicable when for the sake of a few alluring job offers or other false promises about a "guaranteed future," one leaves a country in which the seed for a new and more beautiful life is sprouting, and is already showing the first fruits, for the place that favors a new war and destruction?*
>
> *Is it not an act of political depravity when citizens, whether young people, workers, or members of the intelligentsia, leave and betray what our people have created through common labor in our republic to offer themselves to the American or British secret services or work for the West German factory owners, Junkers, or Militarists? Does not leaving the land of progress for the morass of an historically outdated social order demonstrate political backwardness and blindness?*
>
> *Workers throughout Germany will demand punishment for those who today leave the German Democratic Republic, the strong bastion of the fight for peace, to serve the deadly enemy of the German people, the imperialists and militarists.*

"What is my man reading?" Martina asked. She leaned over the back of the chair, wrapped her arms around my neck, and planted a warm kiss just below my ear. Her long reddish-brown hair draped over my eyes like a curtain.

"I was reading about 1961 until I was savagely attacked by a sex crazed woman."

She stood straight, waved at my head with a playful slap, and sat in the rocking chair opposite me. "What are you smiling at?" she asked.

"You."

"What's funny about me?"

"It's not really you. It's the contrast. You look like a baby with your feet tucked under that baggy robe, the way you cock your head to the side and smile like a little girl, and a week ago Tante Eva sat there. I thought she would wither away before dinner."

Martina examined her nails.

"Anything interesting in the paper?"

"Just how *depraved* it is to want to escape East Germany and how many people died trying. How futile it is to even think about it, and oh yes, a little story about a wall that was built this past year."

She ignored my sarcasm and continued examining her cuticles.

"Timo, you scare me sometimes."

"What do you mean?"

"I think sometimes you want to leave here, too."

I shook the newspaper and opened it to the inside stories shielding my face. "Sometimes, I do."

"Don't you know it's wrong to even think about it? It's treason and punishable to speak about it."

My hands crumpled the paper onto my lap, and I leaned forward.

"Wrong? Is it right to build a wall around people? To punish them for speaking or even thinking?"

Her arms gripped the armrests, and she mirrored my bold, forward posture.

"Timo, grow up! Who knows what's right or wrong? Our parents thought it was right to follow a charismatic nut with a mustache to his doom in a bunker just a few miles from here. The Russians, Americans, French, and English thought it was right to kill innocent people like your parents and then to divide our country up like a loaf of stale bread. The Japanese people thought it was right to crash planes on American soil and kill hundreds of soldiers. Americans thought it was right to drop an atomic bomb murdering and maiming thousands of Japanese citizens. What does *right* even mean?

"What's in my heart. That's what I know. My heart tells me I love where I live and who I am with. What's in your heart, Timo?"

My only response was a blank stare. *Martina,* I thought, *is so smart.*

Exasperated, she sat back hard in her chair. Her smooth, curvy legs shot out from under her robe.

I sat in silence and continued to gaze at her. She no longer looked like the child I had described earlier. She was a mature seductress ... a smart, mature seductress.

"I can't say what's in my heart," I said in a voice just above a whisper, then growing in volume, "but I can tell you what's in my *schwanz.*"

"Oh, no," she screamed, laughed, leaped from her chair, and escaped just before I dove into the empty rocker. We played catch-me-if-you-can all over the house until I finally caught her where we both wanted to be—in her bed.

We made love for hours and didn't speak about escape, politics, or anything of the world outside her bedroom. The darkness outside had engulfed the room during our post lovemaking sleep.

"We'd better get dressed if we want to make it to that party," said Martina.

Our roles at playing *Haus* elevated to an old married couple as we prepared to leave for the New Year's Eve party. She straightened my tie, and I zipped up her cocktail dress.

The party took place in Schönholz, where Martina attended school. Schönholz was another suburb and a few bus stops away on the way to East Berlin. I wasn't excited about attending, since the guests would be her classmate friends and not mine, so I was more than pleased when the bus approached the Schönholz stop and Martina said, "Timo, let's skip the party and ride the bus into East Berlin."

"I thought you wanted to go to this party."

"I did, but now I want to watch the fireworks display at the Brandenburg Gate. I've never seen the *Silvester* fireworks. It would be so romantic."

Along with thousands of Germans standing on both sides of the wall, we stood for hours with our collars up against the biting winter air, but no one seemed to mind the cold. Bottles of beer and mugs of *Glühwein* passed from all directions, and everyone focused upward in drunken anticipation. The first white streaks of aerial bombs shot into the sky ending in loud pops, and everyone cheered the start of the fireworks. For almost an hour, the sky provided the black backdrop to sparkling explosive sprouts of purple, green, blue, red, gold, and color combinations never imagined. For several seconds before the finale, the atmosphere and crowd silenced. The stagnant billows of smoke produced an enormous greyish cloud framed by blackness dotted with bright stars.

During that pause, Martina looked at me and said, "Timo, tell me you'll never leave."

The hazy heavens seemed to clear and so did my mind. I felt the answer to her earlier question, "What's in your heart, Timo?"

I answered Max's and her questions in one statement, "I won't leave here."

Chapter 16

January 2, 1962, 8:20 a.m.

Alex and Wenzel "The Mouse" grumbled in the back of the covered truck as I drove over bumpy, dirt roads inside *Volkspark Friedrichshain*, a spacious urban park east of East Berlin. Max, seated next to me, yelled out the window, "What's the matter, don't you kids like this beautiful nature trail?"

"Fuck you!" Alex said through one of the tiny air holes Max and Sven had drilled in the back of the trailer.

They had also cut much larger holes in the truck bed, so the two men could sweep and shovel dirt that the Becker brothers had emptied into the trailer the previous night.

This started out as a normal day working for *Thomas Schleppen & Transport Company*. We were fulfilling a contract to haul roofing materials: plywood, shingles, and black tarpaper from East Berlin to a building site in Hohenschönhausen, about eight kilometers to the east. But this was also the first day of fulfilling Max's verbal contract of helping the Becker brothers dig their tunnel.

The previous evening the Beckers brought Max into their cellar to inspect their progress. The brothers had told him that they had planned to reach West Berlin "before March and be gone before spring." Max promised, with our help, we'd finish by January 25th. He shook his head when he saw that their tunnel hadn't even reached beneath the middle of their backyard. With some minor changes and fine-tuning of his original plan, he believed we could still meet the promised deadline.

Our mission was to disperse the soil onto dirt roads within the many East German nature parks. We did so on our way to and from our hauling sites. While doing this, two other men from the card club worked in the Beckers' cellar. Sven acted as general foreman there. The women prepared the evening dinner at Max's for everyone. The workers decided that they would switch duties daily to avoid monotony. Max, Sven, and I were the only three who maintained the same jobs every day.

We finished the hauling job just before noon and ate lunch at an outdoor market in East Berlin. The outdoor markets stayed open all year round, and Germans enjoyed eating sausages and drinking beer at these open-air cafes even during winter.

Our daily routine after lunch included a trip through the forest roads surrounding Kindel Lake where Martina and I swam in the summer. On days when our hauling jobs kept us close to home, we would deposit dirt on these rugged paths. On this day and every work day, I'd drive near the water's edge where an abundance of flat stones, most not larger than dinner plates, bordered the shoreline. We gathered a modest number and headed toward the Beckers' house.

I parked in front of the house, and we unloaded the rocks and stacked them forming the start of a stone wall. This provided a cover for parking the truck in front of the Beckers' every night for the next several weeks.

Alex, Wenzel, and Max formed a human chain from the back of the truck to the edge of the Beckers' front lawn. I climbed into the trailer and handed flat stones to Alex. He passed them down the line to Max who stacked the rocks into a small section of a short decorative wall. Since our efforts were just a guise for the real work in the basement, we worked like the soldiers in the *The Bridge on the River Kwai*, an American movie dubbed in German that I had seen a few years earlier. In the film, the Japanese commander of a World War II POW camp ordered British and American captives to build a railway bridge that would benefit Japan's war effort. Knowing the bridge helped the enemy, their early labor consisted of faulty, slow construction interrupted by breaks of playing and diving off the bridge supports.

We joked and kidded while passing the rocks until border guards made their hourly rounds.

"What are you old-timers and the boy doing, constructing your own private graveyard?" said the guard in the passenger side of the military vehicle and both laughed.

Max laughed right with them and said, "Sometimes I feel like that's what I'm always doing. No, these crazy Becker brothers want a decorative wall in front of their house. For what?"

I was so glad Sven wasn't with us. I'm sure he would have goaded the guards and said something like, "Why should we build a decorative wall in their front, when you guards provided such a beautiful wall separating Berlin into two parts in the back?"

The joking guard, a trim athletic looking man in his early twenties got out of the car, jumped into the back of the truck with me and said, "Let me help you, young man," and handed flat stones to Alex.

As they drove off minutes later, Wenzel said, "Sven will love this when we tell him how the guards helped us."

By five-thirty, we, including the Beckers who had returned from their regular jobs, gathered at Max's for a big meal prepared by Helga and Doris. Magda ran her daycare center, so her regular duty would be serving and cleaning up after dinner.

I had expected our tunnel workers to be covered with dirt and sweat, but, although somewhat fatigued, they were clean. The oldest Becker brother's demonstration explained their cleanliness. At his command, his younger brother placed what looked like a miniature table, less than a meter high and wide, on the living room floor.

"Max Thomas, your people did an excellent job today. These men (he pointed toward Sven, Ralf, and Gerhard) made several of these wooden structures," said Erwin.

"They made tables for dwarfs?" asked Helga.

"No, Frau, these are supports we install as we dig. They prevent the tunnel from caving in, and before we eat, we want to see if each of you can crawl through it."

Helga cringed at the thought and waited until last. Everyone before Helga, despite his or her age, made it through on forearms and knees. Helga knelt and poked her huge body between the support legs. The widest part of her body, her hips, fit with a centimeter or two to spare, but as she moved forward her hips knocked at the supports. Breathing hard and red-faced, she emerged and said, "Don't worry. I'll start losing weight tonight and practice crawling every day."

The Beckers looked skeptical.

Sven broke the tension when he said, "Don't worry, men. We'll get her through if we have to grease her thighs with pig fat and hold a chocolate bar in front of her."

Everyone laughed, and we sat down to eat.

I left before dessert to meet Martina at the library. As I closed the door, it occurred to me that I hadn't told Max about my decision to stay.

Chapter 17

January 24, 1962, 10:00 a.m.

Max, Sven, and I rinsed and dried our coffee cups before placing them in Max's cupboard. Sven and I had reported for work as usual, between seven thirty and eight, but Max had only one job for us that day. We had to pick up some light farm equipment in East Berlin around ten thirty and deliver it to a government-run farm about fifty kilometers farther south.

This was Tuesday, and Sunday night the Beckers had held a quiet celebration for all of us working on the tunnel. The project was practically complete. According to their calculations, the tunnel extended beneath the wall and to the edge of the barbed wire fencing on the West Berlin side.

Erwin had raised his beer stein and offered a toast.

"I must admit. I had my doubts whether you old people would be of any help to us. But with your assistance, we finished this tunnel more than a month ahead of schedule. My brothers and I will finish within the next two days. Take a few days off to get your affairs in order, and we will meet Wednesday night at midnight right here and leave Glienicke/Nordbahn, East Berlin, and East Germany forever. *Prost!*"

"*Prost!*" all toasted and touched steins at the table.

Before leaving to deliver the farm equipment, I looked through the work invoices Max kept on his desk in the living room.

"Max, you've contracted jobs all through the summer. Why? You won't even be here," I asked.

He smiled, took the invoices from me, and answered, "Refusing future contracts might lead to suspicion and discovery of the tunnel. Besides, if you decide to take over the business, you'll need the work."

He put the invoices back on the desk, and I turned away from him and headed for the door. During the past weeks, he had never asked what I had decided, and I hadn't told him. I don't know why I couldn't tell him that I was staying. Every time I planned to say it, the words wouldn't come out. Maybe I was afraid. Of what? I couldn't say. Maybe the thought of never seeing Max again stopped me. Maybe deep down I wanted to leave and hadn't truly made up my mind. Maybe the finality of giving up my place in the escape line was too much for me. I never figured out the reason for my silence.

"Timo," Max said to me just before we reached the back door. "We leave tomorrow night. You must have made a decision."

I nodded. Just as before, the words choked me as if they were chunks of dry bread stuck in my throat. My eyes welled, so I looked at my shoes hoping to hide any tears that might escape. I felt my body quake until Max's heavy warm hands rested on my shoulders.

"Never mind, Timo. Just promise me one thing."

Calm now, my moist eyes looked up at him.

"Whatever you've decided, be at the Beckers' Wednesday at midnight. We will either crawl to Frohnau together or say our heartfelt goodbyes then."

We stared at each other for several seconds that seemed like a lifetime until Sven broke the awkward silence.

"Come on little girls, we have work to do," he said and held the door open.

I backed up the flatbed truck, which we hadn't used in weeks because of our dirt dispersing duty, from the backyard drive and into the street. As I pulled forward, we were stopped by a crowd of neighbors standing on the road just a few houses down from Max's.

"Oh, my God," said Sven, "It's the Beckers' house."

I parked the truck, and we ran toward the crowd. The local faction of the *Volkspolizei* (People's Police) had set up the familiar red and white metal barricades used by all East German law enforcement agencies.

"What's going on?" asked Max to the general mass.

"No one seems to know," said an old woman wearing a long heavy coat, boots, and a red babushka. "The police aren't saying. We think maybe one of the Becker brothers is sick or got caught stealing or something."

"I hope that's all it is," I said just loud enough for the three of us to hear.

Max recognized one of the policemen who stood at the far end of the front yard. He and Max attended the same church, so Max walked along the barrier, away from the crowd, and near the policeman.

"Lars," Max said to him as if he didn't want anyone but Lars to hear and motioned with his head to come closer.

Lars, with his arms folded and head down, sauntered toward the barricade. He must have been in his mid to late fifties and close to retirement. Whenever I watched a police action in East Berlin, the older officers always seemed to be assigned away from the crime scene as if they were too old for anything but barrier duty or crowd control. Lars carried his heavy, tall body with a pronounced limp and kept his head down as he approached Max.

"Lars, can you tell me what's happening here?"

The officer lifted his head and stared at Max for a few seconds. He sucked in his cheeks and may have wondered if he should share some confidential information, but anyone who knew Max for any length of time trusted his integrity and discreet nature.

"Well, it seems the Becker brothers built a tunnel under the wall to escape to the West."

Although Max had suspected it, hearing it stunned him, and then another thought hit him. If the Beckers were in custody, they, in a plea deal, might implicate us.

"My God," said Max. "Are they arrested or dead?"

Lars just laughed, looked toward the sky, and said, "No, Max, you don't understand. Four of the brothers work at the ice factory. When they didn't show up for work this morning or call the icehouse, their boss called and asked us to check on them. All five brothers plus twenty-three other people escaped last night."

Lars dropped his head and walked toward the house.

Max, Sven, and I headed back to Max's house in silence. After I shut the front door behind us, Sven screeched, "Bastards!"

Max just said in a low, defeated voice, "I'll call the others" and left the room.

"Make sure you use the code words, 'The card game is off,' and don't let them ask questions, just in case the Stasi are listening," said Sven.

Sven and I sat at the dining room table and perpetuated the silence as if we were at a funeral.

Having informed the others, Max joined us at the table, and Sven asked like a pleading child, "How, Max? How could they betray us after all the work we did for them?"

"You answered your own question before, Sven. They're bastards. And me? I was naïve."

"What do you mean?" I asked.

Max sighed, shook his head, and lay his palms on the table.

"Remember when I told you that Erwin Becker talked in a hushed voice to his brothers in the basement while Simon held a gun on me, and they discussed whether to kill me or to accept my offer of help?"

I nodded.

"They must have decided then that they'd accept our help but leave us in the end."

"Because they didn't want a bunch of old farts clogging up their tunnel," Sven added. "Well, what do we do now?"

Max stood up and said, "We go to work as if nothing happened."

So, we went to work, but not as if nothing had happened. We did our farm equipment job as if a close friend had died, and we were trying to carry on.

It was nightfall by the time we finished. We had dropped off Sven at his apartment building, and I pulled the flatbed next to the house. As I turned off the lights, another set of headlights shined from behind and blinded us like floodlights.

I shaded my eyes and recognized the car. It was a Volga M21, the kind the Stasi drove.

Two men left the car from the front seat. The darkness and blinding headlights made it impossible to make out their features, but the man's voice on the driver's side was all too familiar.

"Timo, come and sit in the car with me. Old man, my friend will escort you into your house and see that you are safe inside," Christian's brother said.

The other man was the brute who had sat in the backseat during my last interrogation. This time, however, he wore a suit and tie like Christian's brother instead of work clothes. He also wore that same smirk on his face. He grabbed Max by the arm and marshaled him inside his house.

"Oh, Timo, Timo, it's a long ride to Stasi headquarters in East Berlin. Do you know that my superiors wanted me to drive you and your boss all the way there to be interviewed? But you know what I told them? I said, 'That's not necessary. The young man is a friend of ours. He helped us crack a defection plot last summer. He'll tell me the truth.' Was I right, Timo?"

"About what? What's this about? What's he doing to Max? If he hurts him, I swear—"

"Calm down, Timo. Nobody will get hurt, and we have respect for old people. All we want is the truth."

As he had done every other time we met, he touched me on the shoulder and gripped it tighter and tighter as he talked.

"About what?" I demanded. I felt my face flushing and anxiety rising within me as I ran my fingers through my hair.

"The neighbors, the Beckers and some of their friends, escaped through a tunnel last night."

"We heard about that."

Loud yelling reverberated from inside Max's house. I couldn't tell if it was Max's voice, the other guy's, or both.

"Yes, you heard, but when did you hear, Timo? What did you hear, and what did you know about that tunnel?"

"What are you saying? That we knew about their tunnel and didn't report it?"

"Not only that, but that you helped them. Other neighbors said they saw your big trailer truck parked in front of the house every day for the past several weeks. It shielded the border patrol on their rounds from seeing the Beckers' activities."

"They contracted us to build a stone wall in front of their house. We didn't know we were blocking the view of their tunnel work."

"How am I supposed to believe that, Timo? The burden of proof is on you. What can you say that—"

Max's front door slammed shut. The other man stomped over to the gate and motioned for Christian's brother to come and talk with him.

"Don't you move," he said and squeezed my shoulder as if it were a rubber ball, left, and joined his partner.

The two men talked for about ten minutes, but it seemed like hours while I sweated inside the Volga.

"Get out," said Christian's brother, and I exited the car.

They entered the car and drove off without another word.

I ran to the front door and couldn't get inside fast enough to find out if Max was okay.

He sat at the dining room table and looked exhausted but relieved. He had already poured himself a shot glass full of whiskey with the dark bottle standing on the table in front of him.

"Get yourself a glass, Timo, and pour yourself a drink. We've earned it."

I did so but couldn't take a sip before knowing what had happened.

"What happened, Max? Why did they let us go? What did you say?"

"The truth."

"What?"

He swigged down his shot of whiskey and poured himself another before continuing.

"Not the whole truth. Just enough to prove our innocence. You see, Timo, the truth sounds different to different ears. I told him that the proof that we knew nothing about the Becker tunnel was that he and his friend were questioning us. If we had known about it, we'd have been in West Berlin by now eating dinner. Somehow, that convinced him, and he convinced his comrade or whatever they call each other."

"Max, that was brilliant," I said and sipped at my whiskey.

"Not entirely. There's always a price we pay for the truth. Now they know our true sentiments and contempt for the state. For me, it's of little risk. I'm an old man, safe and sheltered because of their indifference to the elderly. But they'll be watching you, Timo. At least for a while."

We clinked glasses and drank.

PART III:
RABBITS

Chapter 18

April 12, 1962, 4:30 a.m.

Max sat up in bed. He had had this nightmare about twice a month since Hannah's death. She screams in the henhouse, but Max can't move from his bed to rescue her. This time a real ruckus in the chicken coop awoke him. The chickens squawked in terror.

A fox, he thought. One had killed and eaten several chickens some years earlier when he or Hannah had left the coop door unlatched. *But I'm sure I locked it last night.* Robed but barefoot, he ran toward the small barn and grabbed a shovel on the way.

It had been a long depressing winter. Since the Becker brothers' escape and double-cross, the card club continued to meet monthly, but it wasn't the same. It was as if the Beckers had stolen something from them—maybe their dignity. Despite their rigorous work and youthful spirit, the Beckers' betrayal had sent a cruel message: "You're old and worthless. Did you really think we'd let you old people clog up our tunnel with your frail, slow-moving bodies?" Hearing this message didn't hurt them. They had heard these messages in the words of children and read them in the eyes of young adults since they entered their senior years. But accepting and believing that message damaged them.

They moved slower.

They smiled less.

They aged.

My life also took a downward trend. The dream of running Max's business and living in his house became more distant. Distance. That described much of my life at that time. Martina grew distant. Tante Eva's death in March had ended her parents' Sunday trips to Brandenburg and killed our Sunday rendezvous. Martina spent more and more time in Schönholz with her school friends. She even talked about moving in with an older schoolmate who lived in an apartment there. Only her job at our local library provided opportunities for me to see her.

My sister and brother-in-law's cycle of drinking, working, and fighting remained the only constant in my life. Sometimes, Martina and I had sex at the apartment while Horst and Frieda binged at a tavern, but somehow the thrill and romance of lovemaking fizzled in that pigsty.

Max unlatched the door of the henhouse and stepped inside. Normally, his entrance didn't upset the chickens, but this time it seemed to add to their frenzy. At first, he saw nothing that would have upset them, until it looked as if a clump of the dark brown earth jumped into the air.

"A rabbit? Is that all this is about?"

He opened the door wider to shoo it out with the shovel blade, but when he turned around, it had disappeared. Max got to his knees and peeked underneath a shelf of nests. He spotted a hole just round enough to fit the long-eared creature.

"Sorry, friend," he said, "I'll have to fill your private entrance with dirt and rocks. My chickens don't like you."

Out of curiosity, he went to the back of the chicken house to see where the rabbit had entered but could see no entrance hole or rabbit. The three meters of land between his chicken house and the barbed wire fencing looked flat and unbroken. Between the fence and the wall, the "death zone," he saw nothing, no small hole or animal.

"My God," he said almost loud enough for the guard in the tower to hear. "A West Berlin rabbit."

He jammed the shovel blade into the ground.

Saturday, April 14, 1962

Alex and Wenzel sat opposite each other at one of the card tables while Dora and Sven chatted with the Lehrs in the dining room. Max brought out a tray of drinks.

"Max, you seem a bit nervous tonight," said Dora. "Is something wrong?"

"No, no, it's just that a couple of weeks ago something woke me up, and—"

The Seilers arrived and Ralf said, "Sorry we're late but we had a little car trouble."

"Don't make excuses," said Sven. "We all saw you parked out front and making love in the backseat."

Ralf shook his head and widened his characteristic smile, but Helga slapped Sven on the back of his head.

Dora volunteered to serve during the first several rounds, and they broke up into two teams at each table. As Sven shuffled the cards at one table and Gerhard did the same at the other, Dora said, "Wait. Max was telling us something that happened. Finish your story, Max."

"It was just something that happened in my hen house ..."

He related the story of the rabbit. When he finished, a tense silence followed.

"So," said Sven with a sinister smile, "are you suggesting that if a little rabbit can dig a tunnel about thirty meters long from the West, then why can't a group of, what are we called, senior citizens?"

"No! No! Not again," said Wenzel and stood up. "Haven't we had enough disappointment and humiliation with that Becker tunnel?"

"Hold on, Wenzel. Don't get so excited," Gerhard said and stopped shuffling the cards. "We're just talking. Let's look at the idea rationally. On the plus side, we have experience. As devastating as the Beckers' double-cross was to us, we learned some skills. We learned the mechanics of building such a tunnel, and we learned that we had more abilities than we may have realized. Another positive is that Max's chicken coop is much closer to the wall than the Beckers' house. We wouldn't have to dig as far."

Magda, still self-conscious about speaking to the group, turned toward her husband and said, just to him, but loud enough for all to hear, "Gerhard, I love you, but let's be honest. You're the dreamer in our marriage, and I'm the practical one. Even with the shorter distance, this project would be much more difficult. Since the discovery of the Becker tunnel, security by the border patrol has tightened. They make more rounds now and randomly inspect houses and basements. Yes, we proved we could do some things despite our ages, but the Beckers provided the youthful back strength. You said it yourself, Sven. '... if a rabbit can do it, why can't old people?' The answer is simple. We're not young rabbits."

"But maybe that's our trump card, Magda," Sven said, pounded his fist on the card table, and stood up. The shuffled deck spread across the table and some cards fell to the floor. "Because we're old, no one suspects us. Max has said it many times. They offer the worst insult. They ignore us. They make fun of us behind our backs and to our faces.

Why do you think I needle them with my jokes? It's my way of letting out my anger at their insults.

"Max, in all the random checks of the border houses, have they ever checked your little barn?"

"No."

"No," Sven repeated and sat down. "Who would think that an eighty-one-year-old single man would be digging a tunnel?"

"What about all the materials for the support structures?" added Wenzel. "The four Beckers who worked at the icehouse stole wood pallets from their job for that."

"I still have my construction contacts," said Alex and grabbed the deck of cards from Wenzel who had been reshuffling them. "I can scrounge enough timber, little by little."

"Don't make me go through this again."

Everyone turned toward Helga when they heard her words.

"All of you make fun of me because of my size, and I take it. I even make fun of myself sometimes. But let's face it. I'm probably the reason the Beckers left without us. They didn't think I could make it through, and I've carried that guilt."

She broke down and cried, and Ralf rushed to her side and consoled her.

"No, no, Helga. Don't claim all the credit for the Beckers' swindle. I suspected something from the day I made the deal with them at gunpoint," said Max, "but I was so excited about avenging Hannah's death with my escape that I refused to see it or share my suspicions with all of you. No, Helga, if anyone was to blame it was me. I used all of you, so I could save my life and sweeten the deal with the Beckers by promising your help. I'd never do that again.

"At the same time, look at yourselves. I shared my rabbit story, and right away you start talking about escape. It's still on your minds. Well, it's on my mind, too. I've made plans, for myself, only. I'll not involve any of you. Next week, Maundy Thursday, I'll finish my last hauling contract before my usual month-long break before the summer months. The next day, Good Friday, I plan to start burrowing a tunnel alongside my rabbit friend's. Could I use the help of my human friends? Yes. Are they welcome to escape with me? Of course, but I'm not pressuring you. I'll simply say that I don't plan on hosting another 66-card-playing date.

"Now, let's play cards."

He took the cards, reshuffled and dealt.

Alex turned the wheel of his little two-seater car, and it purred to a stop in the dirt driveway of Wenzel's tiny cedar cottage.

"Coming in for your usual nightcap?" asked Wenzel.

"Of course. We have a lot to discuss."

They hadn't spoken during the short ride from Max's to where Wenzel lived on the northeast end of Glienicke/Nordbahn. Inside the cottage, Wenzel went to his liquor cabinet and poured some sherry into two snifter glasses. Alex stood behind him. They clinked glasses and sipped.

"Well," said Alex as he sat in a dark-upholstered living room chair, "Are we with Max on his escape plan?"

"We've had this discussion before," Wenzel said and remained standing, "about the Becker tunnel. Remember?"

"Yes, and you agreed to go, but for the wrong reason. Sit down. You make me nervous."

Wenzel sat, but remained edgy and said, "I was against it, but I agreed to go because you wanted to go, and with your remark tonight about scrounging wood, it sounds like you're with him again."

Alex set his snifter on a coffee table, lit a cigarette, and said, "I am."

"Then, I guess I am, too, but against my good judgment."

"You idiot, Mouse," Alex coughed out smoke with his response. "That's such a weak answer."

"What do you mean 'weak'? We've had a strong relationship, and that makes for a strong reason to stay together."

The men had been together since their teens. Both were denied an education at a Gymnasium, the most advanced type of German secondary schools, and forced into the working world in 1910.

At the age of fifteen, Alex became a carpenter's apprentice. His skills excelled beyond woodwork, and building contractors sought him out to work on their construction crews. It was cheaper to hire one novice young man who could do the work of a carpenter, plumber, bricklayer, and other tradesmen than to employ five or six seasoned workers.

Wenzel did not adjust as well to the work world. Weak and unskilled, he fumbled at various jobs at his uncle's factory where, after forty years, his status rose only as high as a timekeeper.

"Strong? Strong? Do you call hiding our relationship for over fifty years a sign of strength? Think about it, Wenzel."

Alex sipped his sherry and waited for Wenzel's reaction.

Wenzel nodded. He didn't have to think about it. Paragraph 175 from the 1871 German Empire was still on the books. It was still a crime to be a homosexual in East Germany.

"But, Alex, the law isn't enforced like it was when the Nazis were in charge."

"Oh, no, no. Just because the Soviets didn't confine the likes of 15,000 of us to concentration camps where most died, doesn't mean they don't despise us any less than the Nazis did. You remember those government pamphlets issued to factory workers and construction laborers promoting 'moral reform, masculinity, and the traditional family.' What did they call our way of life? 'Bourgeois decadence' and 'moral weakness.'"

Wenzel looked up at him and pleaded, "We're old and retired, Alex. The Soviets don't care about us. Our own people don't care enough about us to hate us. At least here we have our roots, familiarity, and comfort. Do you think it's that much better for us a few steps beyond the wall in Frohnau, West Berlin, or even anywhere in West Germany? Freedom and democracy haven't extended to the acceptance of us yet. My own Protestant church, through its West Berlin broadcasts, preaches the 'moral weakness' and 'damnation' of homosexuality and the 'piety of the traditional family.'"

Alex set his snifter on the floor and knelt in front of Wenzel. He took the glass from Wenzel's hand, set it down, and held both of Wenzel's hands.

"I've been thinking much about this and reading literature from my underground connections in West Berlin. Once we're beyond that wall, we're not confined to just West Germany. Paris has become much more tolerant of homosexuals. I read where James Baldwin, a Negro homosexual American writer who felt the same persecution in the States, claims he has found utopia in Paris. Wouldn't it be *wunderbar* to live our final years there?"

Wenzel's mouse-like nervousness evaporated. He smiled and nodded.

Ralf stopped the car when they reached the end of their short gravel driveway and turned toward his wife.

"Helga, what's wrong? You've hardly said a word since Max mentioned his tunnel idea, and you seemed to get more and more depressed after each hand of cards. We need to talk about—"

"I don't want to talk about anything. I'm tired and want to go to bed." She slammed the car door behind her and walked to their front door.

Ralf and Helga lived across town from Max in a small cottage like his. Theirs was smaller than Max's, only one story with their bedroom just off the kitchen. An attic, once used as a bedroom, remained empty.

Helga had already retired to their bedroom and shut the door by the time Ralf entered the house. He went to the kitchen cabinet and retrieved his bottle of *Schierker Feuerstein*, a bitter herbal liqueur, poured a few shots into a water glass tumbler, and went into the living room. This had become his Saturday night ritual, especially after the 66 card game.

The kitchen overhead light produced the only illumination in the house. The lighting faded from brightness in the kitchen to dimness in the living room and so did Ralf's mood. He took the small dark wood framed picture from the fireplace mantel and held it. The photo depicted a younger, slimmer Helga guiding a little boy as he learned to ride his first two-wheeled bicycle in their driveway. Ralf smiled. He always enjoyed viewing this picture in the hazy light, but never looked at it when the bright sunshine streamed through the front window.

He returned the photo to the mantel, finished his drink, and went to the bedroom. Helga sat up in bed with the light on.

"I can't sleep," she said in an emotionless tone.

Ralf sat on the bed beside her, touched her hand as if it were glass, and asked, "What is it? Is it about the tunnel?"

She nodded and stared at his hand on top of hers.

"We talked about all this months ago when we had to decide whether or not to be part of the Becker tunnel. Are you still afraid about your size and being able to crawl through? Have you changed your mind about leaving your sister or … Tobias?"

Ralf and Helga had a son, Tobias, who had deserted the Nazi army before the start of the war. He settled in Moscow and joined the Russian military. Even though his parents did not openly support Nazism, the son denounced his heritage and all German ties. During the Russian pillage of Berlin, he fought against his own people, returned to Moscow, married, and rejected all attempts from Helga and Ralf to contact him.

She raised her head and glared at Ralf at the sound of her son's name, but she softened again, shook her head, and said, "No, it's … it's something else. Something I haven't told anyone. Something I had forgotten myself until just a few months ago. Something that happened when I was just a little girl."

Ralf didn't push her. His nickname, The Gentle Giant, evolved from his ability to be patient and quiet while others spoke.

"I told you many times how my parents sent my sister and me to my aunt and uncle's farm in Dennin for two weeks each summer."

He nodded.

"We used to play in an old abandoned farmhouse beyond their cow pasture. One summer we found a dried up well, buried within the tall grasses of an overgrown field behind that house. My sister dared me to get into the water bucket, and she would lower me down by the rope. She promised to crank me back up whenever I wanted. It was a stupid and dangerous challenge, but I was bolder back then and eager to get my older sister's approval. I climbed into the pail, and she lowered me down. With every crank, it grew darker and darker, and I imagined the circular wall around me getting tighter and tighter. I screamed for her to reel me back up. What I didn't know was that she wasn't in full control. I was heavier than she had thought. Instead of winding me down, she struggled just to keep the rope from spinning downward. When there was no rope left and it hung from the crank, I could only see a dot of light above me and complete blackness below. It was a good hour before my aunt and uncle, who had been working in the fields, could come and rescue me.

"For many years after I feared dark enclosed places, but that was a long time ago. Over the years, I thought I had gotten over all that and so I forgot it. But several weeks ago, I was shopping in Alexanderplatz. I got on the U-Bahn (subway) to start coming home. There was a power outage at the station. Everything went dark. People started screaming and packing into the train car. It was so constricted, I couldn't move my arms, and it became harder and harder for me to breathe.

"That's when it all came back to me. I was a little girl again in that well. When they restored the power, the lights came back on, and everyone stared at me. I had been screaming at the top of my lungs, and I was soaked in sweat.

"Don't make me go through that tunnel. If you must go, then leave me, but don't make me go with you."

Ralf held and rocked her as if she were a child and said, "No one is going to make you do anything, and I'm not going without you. Now, lie down and sleep. I'll take care of everything."

He walked toward the wall and switched off the light.

"Dear God," he prayed with eyes closed. "Please show us the way," and he went to bed.

Chapter 19

Sunday, April 15, 1962, 10:40 a.m.

As Max descended the steps with Lars, his widowed police officer friend, a commotion of voices echoed up the short stairwell from the church basement to the sanctuary. After the morning Sunday service, the congregation gathered beneath the chapel for pastries, coffee, and conversation. The basement had once been used for Sunday school, religious instruction for children, but all that had changed when the Soviets took over East Germany in 1949 when I was only four-years-old. My older sister received a Christian Confirmation into a Protestant church at age fourteen. I was subjected to *Jugendweihe* which I called "Atheist Confirmation." Children attended lectures and literature about how to live and to act in a Socialist world devoid of all religious beliefs. The Soviets allowed religious freedom but discouraged children from participating in Christian activities. If the children took part in church functions instead of *Jugendweihe*, both students and teachers bullied them at school. No matter how intelligent these Christian children might be, they were denied a college prep education. Young Christians with vocational skills were blocked from the training that corresponded with their desires and abilities. Consequently, *Jugendweihe* insured that Christianity would expire with its elderly followers.

Max's church exemplified the trend. The small congregation, maybe thirty active members, consisted of no one below the age of fifty. Hannah and Max had socialized with the churchgoing couples. Widows and widowers made up most of the worshipers. Since Hannah's death, Max drank coffee with the widowers which included Lars.

Ralf and Helga attended the same church. Because Helga helped serve coffee and cakes in the kitchen, Ralf often joined one of the single men's tables at coffee hour.

"Ah, the Gentle Giant has chosen to sit with us," Lars said and pulled a metal folding chair near the table for him.

Ralf smiled like a shy schoolboy and sat down.

The men discussed the sermon, sports, and spring chores. In his true introverted character, Ralf kept his comments brief and restricted his communication to polite nods and grins. It seemed to Max as if he had something to say but didn't feel comfortable expressing it.

"You'll excuse me, gentlemen," said Max. "All this talk about spring jobs reminded me of some chores I've been putting off." He slurped the last of his coffee and headed up the stairs.

"Wait," said Ralf, "I'll walk a bit with you."

The two walked the short distance toward Max's house in silence. The leaves on the tree branches that hovered over the road had sprouted, and sunlight danced off their shiny green surfaces. The air still had that slight winter chill that kept the promise of summer in check as they shivered within their lightweight sport coats.

As they neared Max's front yard fence, Max pushed on his wrought iron gate. The loud creaking of metal-against-metal seemed to prompt Ralf. He confronted Max about something, but I couldn't hear his words.

The screeching of those rusty gate hinges, signaled to me that Max had returned from church, and I ran from the kitchen where I had been washing cups, glasses, and plates from the previous night's card club game. Max had given me a key and free use of his house, but I rarely took advantage of it. Despite his generosity, Max enjoyed his privacy, and I respected that.

This Sunday, I needed a friend and the comforts of home. Max and his house remained the closest I had to that. I had just been to Martina's house. We had fought the night before. She wanted to attend a party in Schönholz thrown by one of her school friends. I didn't want to go but relented at her insistence. Martina enjoyed herself. She drank, danced, and flirted. I tried to have fun, but I just didn't fit in well with her friends. I wanted to leave, and she wanted to stay. We argued. I left and waited at the bus stop for her, but she never showed up. When I went to her house this morning, her mother said she had called and stayed at a girlfriend's apartment for the night.

I was losing her.

Max and Ralf appeared to be in a serious conversation. The Gentle Giant looked upset, maybe even crying. Although I couldn't hear their words, Max's soothing tone seemed to calm him. They parted, and I met Max at his front door.

"What's the matter? You lose track of the days?" Max teased. "You're about twenty-four hours early for work."

"I knew you had cards last night and thought an old man like you might need help cleaning up. I was right. That's quite a pile of dirty glasses and dishes."

I tossed a sponge to him.

He caught it and said, "I meant to clean up after church."

"The Gentle Giant seemed a little upset," I said as he washed, and I dried. "Is he okay?"

"I think he'll be all right."

Max appeared to be gaining his youthful spirit again. The Becker tunnel incident had disappointed him but didn't affect him as much as the others—not like Hannah's death had devastated him. Maybe there was truth to that Nietzche saying: "What doesn't kill me, makes me stronger."

"I haven't shared my rabbit story with you," he said as I stacked dishes in the cupboard.

I hadn't seen him for several days. We had worked Monday through Wednesday the previous week. Max tapered off hauling jobs during the spring, so he could take a few weeks off before our busiest season, summer, when construction and farm markets kept us working long hours.

He related the incident from Thursday with the rabbit in his chicken coop. From the way his eyes lit up, I knew where his story led. Something about the idea of leaving Glienicke/Nordbahn and living with Hannah's daughter and grandson in Frohnau must have brought him closer to Hannah.

"So, you're thinking about building another tunnel."

He continued washing the cups and dishes and handing them to me.

"I'm not just thinking about it, Timo. I'm starting work on it this Friday, Good Friday. I'm hoping you'll lend a hand."

"You know you can count on me, Max. Was that what you and Ralf were just talking about?"

Max stared out the back window at the Berlin Wall as he recounted their conversation.

"Ralf told me that Helga had decided not to be a part of our tunnel and escape. She's terrified of small spaces and doesn't know if she can crawl through. You know ... her size ... but he also knows she wants to leave, with all her heart. You know ... with all that had happened with their son. They want a new start. But then he said that he had gotten an idea while he was trying to stay awake," Max said with a laugh because Ralf was also known as "The Sleeping Giant" in church. Sometimes he snored only to be awakened by the sharp elbowing of Helga or laughter from the congregation because of the pastor's jokes about his snoring.

"He said, 'Max, if I promise to work hard every day helping you dig your tunnel, could we build it the size of a doorway?' Timo, the man was fighting back tears, but without much success."

During Max's recollection of his dialogue with Ralf, he had been staring through the kitchen window at the Berlin Wall.

Now, he turned toward me, handed me a rinsed coffee cup, and asked, "What do you think I told him, Timo?"

I dried the cup with a dish towel and said, "That's a lot more work and time, Max. It increases the chances of getting caught."

"I know all that."

"What did you tell him?"

Max's eyes shined like a child's seeing his first brand new bicycle on Christmas morning. "I told him that we'd build a tunnel bigger, better, and faster than those thieving Becker brothers could ever dream of. We'll walk in pairs, comfortably and with dignity, to freedom.

"Timo, my proposition to you is the same as before. You can have my business when I'm gone or join us in the escape. Again, you don't have to—"

"I've already made up my mind this time, Max," I said.

Chapter 20

Wednesday, April 18, 12:15 a.m.

Sven's loud snoring resonated throughout the truck cab. Despite the light rain, I opened my driver's side window to reduce the echo effect. We had parked along the curb at the Heinrich-Heine Strasse border crossing in East Berlin. This would be our last hauling job before the summer season. Max called it "the spring holiday hauling break."

Since the construction of the wall, we were no longer allowed to cross into West Germany for work. Larger companies, however, with offices in both East and West Berlin were permitted to do business in both countries, but only under heavy constraints. AEG, a company that manufactured electrical equipment, was such a company. They had subcontracted us to haul and to deliver materials to a construction site somewhere in Leipzig. We weren't crossing. We were only recipients of the load from West Berlin, so we didn't have to endure the customs procedure. One of the restrictions was that companies wanting to cross the border from the West had to make an appointment with the border patrol, produce the necessary documentation, and submit to a thorough search. The Soviets discouraged these intercity companies from functioning by scheduling crossings at inconvenient times of the day and night, demanding painstaking written verifications, and subjecting drivers to detailed searches of their truck, cargo, and sometimes their bodies.

The border guard tapped on the passenger's side window and asked, "Why are you parked here?"

Sven, startled at first, awoke and straightened up. When he saw the uniformed officer, he grinned, adjusted his flat cap, and rolled down his window.

"We're expecting a large shipment of cow dung from Munich. Search through it well. We heard the cows ate some gold nuggets by mistake."

"Don't get smart, old man. I could have you arrested."

"Come on, smile. I was just joking. We're waiting for an AEG truck from the other side. There aren't any gold nuggets, but when they dump the shipment in front of your crossing gate, we could use some help shoveling it into our truck. Timo, do we have an extra shovel in back?"

The officer just shook his head and walked back to his post.

Again, Sven's sarcasm made me nervous. The guard was right. He could trump up a charge and have us arrested, but Sven always knew just how far to go with his mockery. He seasoned his humor like a master chef with just the right amount of spices to get his desired result.

He rolled his window up again and slumbered back to sleep.

Unable to nap, I marveled at this break in the Berlin Wall. It stopped several meters on each side of Heinrich-Heine Strasse, a wide street leading into West Berlin, as if God had cut a piece of the wall out and tossed it into space. Huge guard towers loomed on each side of the road. Below each tower, guards checked vehicles coming and going across the border. Two red and white striped crossing gates in the downward position blocked traffic. Beyond the gates, several low wooden barriers created a maze, so that vehicles allowed to pass had to go slow enough to avoid crashing into the barriers before crossing from one side to the other.

My eyes started to close, but a rumbling noise awakened me. I recognized the sound of a heavy loaded truck fighting against its weight as the driver went through the gears to gain speed. An AEG truck passed us on our side of the wall heading for West Berlin. Rather than slowing as it approached the crossing guards, it had reached top speed and crashed through the gate poles as if they were toothpicks.

We jumped out of the cab and watched as gunfire flashed and crackled through the darkness from the guard towers. The truck crunched the wooden barriers beyond the gates but crashed into the brick wall of a building on the West Berlin side. Moments later, the truck burst into flames.

A guard ran toward us with his weapon drawn and demanded, "What do you know about this?"

I put my hands in the air and said, "Nothing. We were waiting for a pickup from the other side."

The guard turned toward Sven who nodded his agreement and raised his hands, too.

"Get out of here," he said and must have thought, *why would these two idiots hang around to watch and risk arrest if they were part of this crime?*

"But what about our pickup from the West?" asked Sven.

"There'll be no more crossings tonight. Get moving!"

The previous Sunday I had told Max that I would not only help him build his tunnel, but also, I wanted to escape with him. When I later learned about the details of what we had just witnessed, I began to doubt my decision to leave.

I turned the truck around and drove us home.

I didn't wake up until late that Wednesday afternoon. All night I dreamt about that truck crashing through the border crossing. In the dream, I drove the vehicle. The truck headed straight toward the crossing gates. I tried to stop it, but every time my foot hit the brake pedal, the truck accelerated. Sven laughed and screamed insults at the guards as we crashed through the barriers. The guards fired at us but couldn't seem to hit us. We headed straight for a brick wall, and I awoke before impact.

The apartment was empty. Frieda and Horst were either at work or at a tavern after their shift. The kitchen clock read 3:25 p.m. I made some coffee and ate a stale *Berliner* (jelly donut) from the bread box. Frieda had left a note on the kitchen table saying that Max had called before they left for work. He said that he rescheduled the AEG pickup for that evening, and Sven would pick me up around five o'clock.

I dressed and tuned our little portable TV set to the West Berlin station. I hated East German television shows. The government infused every program with political propaganda. Our high-rise apartment building complex had a shared antenna on the roof, so every set could get the East German stations as clear as if the broadcasts were next door. When alone, I'd disconnect the receiver wire from the wall connection and reconnect it to the rabbit ears antennae above our set. By manipulating the antennae probes I could receive West Berlin TV programs—fuzzy, but preferable to the East German garbage shows.

During the 60s, German teens enjoyed American Westerns dubbed and rebroadcast throughout Europe. My favorite was called *Gunsmoke*. I had an adolescent crush on the Miss Kitty character.

After the *Gunsmoke* episode, a stone-faced announcer appeared and stated the headlines for an afternoon news program: "A young man dies driving to freedom ..."

That opening headline captivated me, but I had to endure about ten minutes of stupid commercials. That's how all German television stations handled commercials. They never interrupted programs but aired them before and after the shows.

Following the advertisements, a long shot of a newsroom set zoomed in on the news announcer seated at a desk. Behind him was an enlarged photograph of a young man who looked not much older than

I. He had a shy, innocent expression, and his eyes looked somewhere beyond the camera lens as if searching for something or someone.

The essential story was this:

> *Klaus Brueske drove a truck for AEG where his father also worked. The company operated between East and West Berlin. When the border was sealed on August 13, 1961, his father chose to remain in West Berlin, but Klaus Brueske stayed in the East with that AEG office.*
>
> *He borrowed a truck from the company on Tuesday, claiming that he needed it to move. He loaded the truck cab with sand and gravel to increase the vehicle's ability to break through the barriers at the border patrol checkpoint.*
>
> *That evening he met his seven friends in a bar. Peter G., one of the surviving young men, told authorities that they had spent their last East German money getting drunk "in an atmosphere of morbid humor." They agreed to separate for a while and meet at the truck again later that night. Only three of them showed up. Klaus Brueske sat at the wheel, Lothar M. was in the passenger seat next to him, and Peter G. lay down on the back of the fully-loaded truck platform.*
>
> *After midnight, the young men raced through the first and second barriers. Border guards fired fourteen shots at them. The vehicle continued to speed across the border, until it hit the wall of an apartment building on the West Berlin side. The three were rushed to Urban Hospital and treated. Two survived, but Klaus Brueske died. Two shots through the back of his neck caused him to lose control of the vehicle but didn't kill him. Upon impact with the wall, he was buried in sand and suffocated to a painful death.*

The newsman moved on to other stories, but I fixated on that one. The photo of that young man imprinted on my brain, and I turned off the TV. My face must have looked similar to his when I told Max I wanted to escape through his tunnel.

Why did I want to escape? What had changed my mind?

Martina—that was the reason. I hadn't tried to contact her since Sunday when I discovered she had stayed in Schönholz after the party. I wasn't escaping East Germany. I was escaping from our breakup, *or was it a breakup? Maybe I still loved her. Maybe she still loved me.*

My head ached.

That's when someone knocked on the door. Part of me prayed that it was Martina, but it was only Sven.

"Ready to begin our last job for *Thomas Schleppen & Transport Company*?" he, carrying a rolled-up newspaper under his arm, asked and headed for our refrigerator. "Will your sister or brother-in-law miss one bottle of beer from their stockpile in here?"

"They would if they stayed sober long enough to count, so don't worry about it."

He opened a kitchen drawer, looked for a bottle opener, and tossed the newspaper on the table.

"Did you read about what we witnessed last night?"

"No," I said and picked up the paper, "but I saw it covered on West Berlin television."

The front page of *Neues Deutschland* reported the incident with a Soviet twist:

> *On April 18, 1962 a certain Klaus Brueske was shot and killed while violently breaking through the border crossing at Heinrich-Heine Strasse. His act placed the lives of members of the border security in extreme danger. An investigation revealed that the shooting was justifiable. It*

was an especially glaring example of border breaching. The incident has prompted the military to install more formidable secondary barriers beyond the main gate.

There was no mention of the two escapees or Klaus Brueske's background.

We sat at the kitchen table, and I filled Sven in on the West Berlin broadcast version.

"It doesn't surprise me that an East Berlin newspaper cut out the escape and reported an angle sympathetic to the government," he said and took a swig of his beer.

I observed Sven. *Here is a man*, I thought, *in his seventies with a beautiful girlfriend, Dora. They both want to pull up their roots and escape to the West.*

"Sven, why do you want to leave here?"

He almost choked on his beer when he laughed at my question.

"That's funny. You ask, 'why do you want to leave here?' I don't want to leave here. I want to escape. There's a difference."

My confused look must have prompted him to elaborate.

"It's hard to explain, Timo. I *feel* what I mean, but it's difficult to put it into words. You see, I love Germany, but Germany is not just a place on the map. It's ... It's ..."

It reminded me of an expression Martina used, and I said, "A state of mind?"

"Yes, that's it. I've heard young people talk about a Soviet state of mind, but I guess you could call it a German state of mind. Timo, do you have dreams? I don't mean those crazy things that go on inside our heads when we sleep. I'm talking about waking dreams."

He offered me a drink of his beer, and I took it while thinking about his question. I thought about my former dream, my fantasy of living in Max's house with Martina and running the hauling business, and my habit of using my fingers like a comb through my hair returned. It signaled to me, and maybe to Sven, too, that the question made me feel uncomfortable.

"No, not anymore," I said.

"Dreams are why you want to escape. I grew up under the Reichstag government. I always felt the freedom to dream. Even under the Nazis, Hitler couldn't stop me from dreaming. But under these Soviets, this communism—"

"You mean socialism."

"No!" he said and slammed his hand on the table. "That's what they've drummed into the heads of you younger people. It's not socialism. True socialism is not a bad thing. You pay a little more to the government, so the government can take care of your basic needs: health costs, welfare, roads. But you're free to work hard and to make something of yourself, to earn extras for you and your family. You can still dream. With communism, everything goes to the government. Yes, they, too, take care of your needs, but everyone makes the same money no matter how hard they work. Everyone but the leaders are workers. No one can aspire to anything higher. With communism there are no dreams.

"Timo, Dora and I are dreamers. Once we were young dreamers. We dreamt of owning our own tavern. Dora would have been the perfect barmaid/hostess, and I would be the joke-telling bartender who still has fix-it skills to keep the establishment running. We may be too old to fulfill our dreams, but we're never too old to dream. Remember that, Timo."

I stopped using my hands as combs and clasped them in front of me as if in prayer. His reasoning made sense to me, but another question evolved, and I had to ask it.

"Sven, I know how close you and Dora are, but just imagine that you wanted to escape, and she wanted to stay. What would you do?"

He stared at the beer bottle and peeled at the label with his thumbs, almost as if his answer was somewhere on that brown glass.

"That's a good question, Timo. Does one follow his dreams or his heart when the two are in conflict? I can't answer that without much thought. It would be a difficult decision, but why do you ask?"

I looked down at my folded hands.

His attention shifted from the beer bottle, and he focused on me.

"Is it your girlfriend here? Are you still in love with her?"

I nodded and spoke like a child admitting guilt, "Maybe … I don't know."

"Well, Timo, no one can answer your question but you. It's a tough decision, the kind adults must make for themselves."

I felt more confused now than ever but managed to say, "But I can't stay now even if I wanted to. I've already told Max I was going."

"He knows you might change your mind."

"How?"

Sven took a long drink of his beer before answering.

"Believe it or not, Timo, Max was once a young man, too."

I nodded and smiled, acknowledging that I often forgot that about him.

"There's one other thing that frightens me, Sven. Even if I have nothing to keep me in East Berlin and I cross the border, what will I do and where will I go?"

"You'll do whatever you want and go wherever you please."

Chapter 21

Wednesday, April 18, 6 p.m.

Gerhard and Magda Lehrs stood outside *der Tränenpalast* (The Palace of Tears) with Professor Dieter Strauss, Gerhard's former colleague and protégé from Humboldt University.

The Palace of Tears didn't look much like a real palace, but the tears were real. It was a customs border crossing at the East Berlin Friedrichstraße train station, where East Germans said goodbye to West Berlin visitors. The glassed-in structure with a semi-circular front had only been created that year. Only travelers from West Berlin used this border crossing. East Germans were forbidden to travel via the trains to the West.

Professor Strauss turned toward Gerhard and Magda. Although two heads taller and as many decades younger than his hosts, he looked up to Gerhard with the reverence and respect of a novice musician to his maestro. Strauss presented a striking figure with his towering, slim physique filling out his tailored three-piece blue suit. Gerhard often described him as resembling Osker Werner, a popular Austrian actor of international fame during the 60s. Strauss offered a smile and a firm handshake to both as he spoke.

"Well, *danke* for your warm hospitality."

"It's too bad you couldn't spend more time with us, Dieter," said Magda.

"I would have loved to, Magda. I enjoyed the dinner and sparkling conversation, but I now have family on the other side and need to be with them over the Easter holiday." He stepped closer and lowered his voice. "Remember, Gerhard, I can get you a part-time or even a full-time adjunct position in our School of the Humanities. The Free University of Berlin would be proud to have my mentor, Dr. Gerhard Lehrs, in the Literature Department."

Gerhard beamed at hearing his name associated with The Free University of Berlin, and clasped Dieter's handshake with both hands. The university had become world famous for its research in the humanities, social sciences, and natural and life sciences. It evolved in West Berlin during the Cold War as Communists gained control of Humboldt University in East Berlin where Gerhard had taught and Dieter interned under him. Dieter defected to West Berlin. Gerhard stayed. He had loved Humboldt University and relished his prestige as a respected scholar. By the time he realized that the Soviets had stripped him of his status and free intellectual thought and speech, it was too late to defect.

Gerhard smiled and said, "I'll remember that. You just never know."

Dieter tipped his hat to both and entered the *Tränenpalast*.

Neither Gerhard nor Magda had mentioned Max's escape plan to him. It wasn't that they didn't trust Dieter, but sometimes escape plans just leaked out. For example, in passing, Dieter might say to a colleague that they could be getting a new professor and that could start an investigation.

Unlike "The Palace of Tears," an atmosphere of joy filled the area. Most people were arriving from West Berlin to be with relatives for the Easter weekend. Gerhard and Magda moved to the side of the glass building, away from the crowd. They watched Dieter stand in line to be interrogated and searched.

"I didn't tell you this, but on my way here to pick up Dieter this morning I gave Ralf and Helga a ride to the farm market," said Gerhard.

"Oh?"

"They've decided to help Max and to escape, too."

She turned toward him and spoke as if disciplining a child at her daycare center.

"Gerhard, if you think telling me that the others are going will force me to make up my mind, you're wrong. I told you why I wasn't sure I wanted to escape this time. I still feel guilty because I did so little to help with the Becker tunnel."

"Everyone knew that you had to work all day with the children, you did help with dinner at Max's every night. Anyway, there'll be much more work on Max's tunnel. Ralf convinced him to make it tall enough for people to walk through—much more dirt to dig and to dispose of."

Through the glass, they watched security personnel checking the contents of luggage. A guard searched the handbag of a little girl and her mother before they entered the interrogation area. He pulled out a rather large rag doll and placed it on the counter. He felt the doll's body as if he were a doctor examining a patient and then frowned. The little girl cried when he ripped open the doll with a pocketknife and pulled out a bottle of liquor and several garden vegetables, perhaps used as padding for the bottle. He gave the torn doll back to the little girl, confiscated the contents, and scolded the mother before leading them into the debriefing room marked: INTERROGATION.

A few minutes later, Dieter entered the interview room.

Magda seemed to be in a daze for several seconds before she blocked Gerhard's view and said, "I have an outrageous idea!"

She turned and waved again at Dieter, but he had disappeared behind the closed door.

Thursday, April 19, 6:17 a.m.

As soon as I walked outside our apartment building, Christian's brother grabbed my arm. He blew out a cloud of ash colored smoke and seemed to speak to anyone passing by.

"Another beautiful morning. How about I give you a ride to work, Timo?"

It had been months since he and his Stasi friend drove away from Max's that night. I had nearly forgotten about Christian's brother and convinced myself he'd never bother me again. This was the day of Max's meeting with his friends about the tunnel plans.

Of all days, I couldn't let him drive me there, or did the Stasi already know about the tunnel idea? What the hell did he want now?

My hands began to sweat.

"No, *danke*, as you said, it's a beautiful morning. I'll walk."

"Then let's talk. That's not a question. It's an order."

He ushered me toward his parked car, and I took my usual position in the front passenger's seat and peeked into the backseat area. We were alone this time.

"Now, let's see, the last time we talked like this was some months ago at night in front of your boss's house. My friend convinced me that you and your boss knew nothing of the Becker tunnel. Your boss used as proof the fact that both of you didn't leave, but would have, had you known about it. But you know what I said, Timo? I said, 'Well, maybe that tired old man would have escaped, but not Timo. Timo is loyal to his state. He's helped us before. He would have alerted us about the Beckers if he knew.' I was right wasn't I, Timo?"

I sat in silence for about a minute before speaking. I stopped myself from running my fingers through my hair, because I had come to recognize that this was a noticeable habit that signaled my discomfort.

"What do you want now? Neither Max nor I have done anything wrong."

"Exactly. We're not worried about you, your boss, or any of his ancient friends—except for one, Professor Gerhard Lehrs."

"I hardly know him. I hardly know any of Max's friends or what they do except play cards once a month."

"But you are very close to your boss, Max Thomas, and he trusts you. Ask him about Professor Lehrs."

"Why? What do you want to know?'

His familiar habit of massaging my shoulder returned, as he said, "We normally don't tell our NVA recruits—"

"I'm not officially a National People's Army recruit," I said, but he continued as if he hadn't heard me."

"… details about our investigations, but I like you, Timo, and trust you.

"Professor Lehrs was asked to retire some years ago from his position at Humboldt University because of his, let us say 'unpopular' political views. One of his former colleagues who shared his views, defected to a university in West Berlin. He recently visited the Lehrs. We suspect he may have offered him a position in the West and encouraged him to defect. All we want to know is if any of it is true."

"I don't know. I don't like being an informer."

This seemed to irritate the interrogator. He gripped the steering wheel, took a deep breath, and then smiled before saying, "Yes, but you do like your sweet girlfriend. What's her name? Martina?"

His message was clear. It was a threat. He was suggesting assaulting her like they assaulted my sister, but I had a surprise for him, or thought I did.

"Well, she may not be my girlfriend anymore. We may have broken up."

This didn't seem to faze him. His smile evolved into a laugh. He tapped me on the knee and said, "Ahh, don't worry, Timo. It's springtime, and they say both flowers and young love grow wild during this season. All will be well. Now, get to your job and keep your ears open. I'll be in touch."

PART IV:
THE SENIORS' TUNNEL

Chapter 22

Thursday, April 19, 9:30 a.m.

Max's dining room table looked the same as it had months earlier when the card club met to discuss the plan for the Becker tunnel, but this was different. It was their tunnel, *Der Seniorentunnel*.

As Max had expected, all had shown up again.

I sat in a chair outside of the group and served coffee at anyone's request.

Max took his position at the head of the table with a stack of papers in front of him. At some point, he leaned forward and spoke, as if he were the CEO of a big company and addressing his board of directors.

"*Hallo*, my friends. Well, we're going to try it again, but this time, we are in charge. Exactly twenty days from tomorrow we will be on the other side of that goddamned wall."

Dora stood, clapped, and led the others in an ovation.

"Sven has already used his electrical skills and installed a security system. Sven?"

Sven rose from his chair and walked to the front window. He flicked on an innocuous light switch on the wall.

"In the upper corner of Max's chicken coop, a single light bulb is on. I can extend a series of lights from there as our tunnel gets longer. One flash means the border guards are making their usual rounds up the street, and we are to stop working and remain quiet. Two flashes, we can resume. Three flashes, someone is approaching the chicken coop, and we should close up the operation temporarily which we'll explain later."

"Good job, Sven," said Wenzel. He raised his coffee cup offering a toast, but no one followed.

"But expect that we'll have other obstacles to overcome along the way," added Max. "One that concerns me now is the dirt displacement."

"What's the problem?" asked Alex. "I don't think there'll be that much more. Yes, our tunnel will have a higher and wider passageway than the Beckers', but your chicken house is much closer to the wall. Ours will be shorter."

"It's not the amount of dirt that worries me, Alex. It's where we leave it."

"What's wrong with sweeping it onto the forest roads through the holes in the bottom of your truck—the way we did it before?" Wenzel asked. His question was for Max, but he focused on Alex, seated across from him, for approval. Alex gave him a nod as if to say, "Excellent question."

"Maybe nothing. Maybe everything," said Max. "After they discovered the Becker tunnel, we don't know how much post investigation went on. They may have been curious as to how they disposed of the soil and discovered the extra dirt on the forest roads which means they'll be watching for that again. Also, it's known that I suspend my hauling contracts for several weeks in the spring. If I get stopped while in route of getting rid of the dirt, I can't use the excuse that I'm in some distant town because I'm on a job. I'm not worried about people seeing me driving around town or nearby because they are used to seeing me use my truck for errands, social visits and—"

"I think I have a solution for that," said Magda.

Her face reddened as everyone focused on her. During the card club meetings, she kept to herself most of the time except for polite conversation. This was the first time she had addressed the whole group. Her slight frame shook a little as she rose and spoke.

"I know I wasn't much help with the other tunnel."

Volleys of comments such as, "We know you worked during the day" and "You helped clean up after dinner" attempted to quell her concern, but she waved them off and continued.

"No, no, my point is that I think I have a pretty good plan for disposing of the dirt."

Max sat down and yielded the floor to her, and everyone concentrated on Magda and her words.

"As you all know, I run the Glienicke/Nordbahn daycare center. We are not just a babysitter. The government insists that we are an educational institution, too. They check on us on the third Monday of each month. Our last evaluation was just a few days ago. The state evaluator gave us our usual assessment—high marks for our programs that teach basic arithmetic, applied science, and urban living, but poor rankings for not fostering the learning of natural science and rural living. They even threatened to take us over if we didn't show improvement soon. We don't have the resources to take the children on fieldtrips to local farms or purchase more educational materials, but we do have our large vacant area to use for the children's recreation. I thought maybe we could use the dirt to create a miniature farm where the children could grow vegetables and raise small animals. Maybe Max could donate some of his chickens."

"That's brilliant," Helga said and waved as a signal for me to fill her coffee cup, "but won't the border patrol or your evaluator be suspicious of where all that soil came from?"

"The border patrol never pays attention to us. Evidently, they must figure little children are not capable of escape."

"Funny, isn't it? When it comes to defecting, no one pays attention to young children and us old adults," Gerhard said and beamed at his wife's plan as well as her hidden ability to speak in public. With his coffee cup in hand, he gestured for her to carry on.

"And our next evaluation won't be until May 21st. According to Max, we'll be gone weeks before that time." Magda said and wiped a tear from her eye before she added, "And the children will have that little farm to remember me when I've gone."

Helga reached over and hugged her.

"Well," Max said and sat back with a look of relief, "that takes care of one major problem. *Danke*, Magda.

"Now, our work will start each morning at nine. We'll follow a similar schedule and assignment of duties as we did with the Becker tunnel. I'll need three people working in the chicken house at all times and at least two people in the house to monitor the security light and to prepare refreshments and meals. I will be working and supervising in either the chicken coop or the house. Timo will drive the truck and supervise the dirt disposal. Just like before, the rest of you can decide each day which duties you'd like to perform. We can switch or stay on assignments, either way is fine as long as all jobs are covered, and we're all content."

"You mentioned a schedule," said Wenzel. "Do we have a regular schedule of what we want to accomplish each day?"

"Good question," answered Max, and he picked up the stack of papers in front of him, tapped them together to align them, and turned to me. "These are the daily schedules. Timo, take this stack and lock it in the safe."

I could only imagine the dumbfounded looks on their faces as I took the papers up to the master bedroom where the safe was concealed behind a portrait of Hannah. Max knew they might feel betrayed that he didn't share the details of the overall plan, but he also knew that even if one sheet was discovered by anyone outside the group, it could lead to tragedy.

"I'm sorry," he said, "but this stack will not leave that safe again. There are twenty sheets, and each sheet diagrams our tunnel challenge for that day. I can tell you this, the first page outlines the building of the entranceway and the concealment hatch. The last one shows the exit way. The eighteen pages between show an estimate of about two meters of tunnel construction per day. That even allows for Sundays off and some delays for unforeseen problems, and we should be out by midnight, May 9th. Each day, we will start at this table at nine. I'll share the page for that day with you here, and we will discuss the job. Following that, the paper will be burned in that fireplace."

A short silence preceded Alex's question, "When do we start?"

"Tomorrow, Good Friday."

They talked and planned for hours afterward. Alex sat next to Max and picked Max's brain as he wrote notes on a legal pad. They looked like two young contractors going over an important building scheme. Helga and Dora discussed meals and made up a long grocery list. Magda sat near them, sketched out the area behind her day care center, and planned her children's farm. Sven fine-tuned his security system and brought more wire and single-bulb fixtures out to the chicken coop. Wenzel hopped from group to group like a little mouse offering suggestions, questions, and comments.

It was fun to watch these older people behaving in such a vibrant and excited manner. I left and thought about the adventurous thrill of escaping … until I reached the door of my apartment building.

Martina sat about five or six steps up the stairwell inside the main entrance. She wore a mini-skirt, nylons, black flat shoes, and a light blue spring windbreaker. Her hair hung over her left shoulder as she cocked her head and exposed a small pearl-like earring on a short, thin chain.

My pride kept me from running up the stairs and hugging her. Instead, I stood and asked, "What do you want?"

"You. I've missed you, Timo."

The words "I've missed you, too" choked inside me.

She descended the stairs, took my hand, and led me out the doorway.

"Come. Walk with me to work, and we can talk."

We took the forest path toward town. Neither of us spoke, but the woods and warming spring air provided reminders of how we had used this forest and summer to nurture our relationship. Our eyes focused on the brown sign with the carved-in-yellow-painted arrow indicating the connecting trail to Kindel Lake, where we lost our virginity.

She broke the silence and said, "I'm sorry for the way I acted."

"Me, too. I mean, not just for the way you acted, but for my behavior, too. I don't know. When you're with your school friends you're different, and I feel … out of place."

She stopped walking and took both my hands in hers, but she wouldn't look into my eyes. Her eyes transfixed on the patch of dirt, the path between us.

"I know. I know. Things are changing. I'm very confused right now, but that doesn't mean I don't love you and want to be with you."

"I'm confused, too. There are many things on my mind right now. Some things I haven't been able to mention like…"

She dropped my hands and looked up at me.

I realized that I had almost said too much—almost blurted out about the tunnel, Max's offer, and Christian's brother.

"Just about my future, maybe our future. You know, whether I should go back to school, work, find new work, join the military, or even become a border guard like your brother keeps pushing."

She smiled at this, and we continued walking.

"There are some things you should know if we are to continue our relationship. I'm leaving Glienicke/Nordbahn and moving in with my friend, Greta. She has an apartment in Schönholz. I'll be closer to school. I'll also be quitting my job here and looking for part-time work there."

We had reached the library steps.

She took both my hands again and searched my eyes for a reaction, but there was none. Somewhere in the back of my mind, I had seen this coming and expected it. Only one question remained. Was this the end or a new beginning?

"Timo, I still love you and want to keep seeing you."

Her arms hugged my neck, and we shared a long kiss. She shook a little and stepped back as if something inside her was about to implode.

"There's something else, Timo. I think I might be pregnant."

Her voice cracked, and tears flowed down her face.

Chapter 23

Friday, April 20, 10:45 a.m.

Our first day of tunnel construction began over an hour late. Max wanted to give himself and the others the opportunity to attend morning Good Friday church services. They all sat at the dining room table chattering and drinking coffee.

I welcomed the extra hour of sleep. Thinking about Martina's return and her possible pregnancy kept me awake most of the night, but I awoke with a fresh attitude. I felt free. Maybe I had learned something from all the anxiety I had experienced over my decision either to escape or to stay during the Becker tunnel ... or maybe I was just maturing. Worry and fear seemed pointless, neither influenced the outcome. Fate dictated my future, and I would accept my destiny either way. If Martina was pregnant, we would marry, live in Max's house, and I would run the hauling business. If not, I would defer my decision to leave or to stay as long as I wanted, maybe right up until the day of the exodus. In the meantime, I would bury myself in the work of building that tunnel for the happiness of Max and his friends. It was as if a heavy boulder had converted into a helium balloon and floated from my aching shoulders and upward into space.

Only one thought threatened me—The Stasi. Christian's brother might be pestering me to get information about the Lehrs. That was nothing compared to my knowledge about the tunnel, but I locked that wisdom inside of me and kept it there. In twenty days, it would all be over. I'd either be in West Berlin or living in Max's house and running his business. Of course, there's a good chance that the Stasi wouldn't believe that I knew nothing about the tunnel if I stayed, but I had almost three weeks to work on that problem.

"Timo, get the first sheet from the safe," said Max.

He beamed when I pulled it from my windbreaker pocket. My efficiency must have pleased him.

"This is our work for today," he continued and held the sheet of paper up for all to see. "I'll pass this around for you all to get a closer look, but first let me explain. This is a diagram of the inside of my chicken house."

He used a pencil to point as he spoke. Max had a knack for mechanical drawing. The sketch depicted a clear view of the walls, floor and ceiling from the vantage point of just inside the doorway. Above the sketch, he noted: 4 m. X 5m. X 2.5 m. to depict the dimensions. In the center of the floor, he had drawn a square with what looked like a box in the middle of it. Below the square, a dotted line formed a cubicle beneath the floor.

"Most of you have at some time seen the inside of my henhouse, much to the displeasure of my chickens. You know that it's a dirt floor. The square represents the cement slab in the middle, and the box represents the little wood stove Hannah made me put it in there, so the chickens wouldn't be cold in the winter despite my insistence that chickens naturally stay warm."

Several of us grinned as we remembered Hannah's love of animals.

"Both the stove and the slab are easily moved with the help of two people. The slab is about one-and-a quarter meters square. Today beneath the slab," he pointed to the dotted line, "we'll dig a hole, one-meter square and four meters deep and insert a sturdy ladder down it. Then we'll recover the hole with the slab and stove and eat a hearty meal."

Gerhard spoke while the sheet passed around.

"Max, how did you come up with the dimensions for the hole?"

"Actually, our construction expert came up with those figures. Why don't you explain it, Alex?"

Alex rocked back on his chair and said, "Well, first, any one of us can comfortably fit down a meter-square hole."

"Thank you," said Helga and patted her belly to several titters of laughter.

"But figuring the depth is trickier. We need roughly one and three-quarters meter height for us to walk upright through the tunnel. We also need at least two and a half meters above us. If we go much deeper, we may run into a sewage line or a well. Also, the weight of the earth above us might be too much for the supports we build. If we don't make it deep enough, we might run into a water main, utility lines, sunken wall supports, or thick tree roots. We still might run into problems at that depth, but a hole that deep diminishes those risks considerably."

Wenzel patted his partner's shoulders.

"Okay," Max continued, "Alex and Timo will pick up some lumber today. I'll need at least two of you in the house at all times to operate the security system, answer calls, and prepare food and drink."

"That'll be me and Dora," said Helga.

"Ralf, Wenzel, Gerhard, Sven, and I will be in the chicken house working in shifts—pickaxing and digging the hole."

I performed what would become the daily ritual. After everyone had a chance to peruse the worksheet, I took it to the fireplace, lit it with a match from the mantel, and threw it into the hearth.

We split up and got to work.

Alex had worked almost fifty years all over Germany in the construction business before retiring. Although many of his building cohorts had also retired, he still maintained many contacts in the business. We drove in the covered trailer truck to a site near the Alexanderplatz train station in East Berlin. Construction crews had torn down an apartment building built before the war. They were rebuilding it, so the apartments were smaller, uglier, and less comfortable—much like the apartment complex where I lived.

I sat in the cab while Alex donned a yellow hardhat at the construction office/trailer and talked to a foreman on the site. They laughed and slapped each other's backs for a while before Alex motioned for me to back up the truck. The foreman ordered some workers around my age to throw some two-by-fours and plywood planks into the back.

"Nice fellow," said Alex as he boarded the cab with me and waited for them to load the truck.

"So, what did you say to this guy?" I asked.

"I told him I was building a little live-in addition over my garage. We construction men are always doing small projects like that and using scrap materials for it. It's not an unusual request from a retired worker, so it doesn't raise any suspicion. It also helps the company get rid of leftover pieces they can't use again."

I nodded my approval of his plan and gripped the steering wheel, but an obvious question occurred to me.

"Shouldn't we get all the lumber at once for the whole tunnel?"

"No, we'll hit a different construction site every other day and get just enough wood for a few days. That way we won't raise suspicion from the foreman, and Max won't attract attention from his neighbors or the border police with a pile of raw lumber lying outside."

I smiled and said, "Old people are smarter than they look."

"We've had more time to learn than you juvenile delinquents," he said.

A few years earlier, I had harbored a curious suspicion, maybe even a distaste for Alex. Germans didn't talk much about homosexuality back then. Eccentricity was offensive, and fitting in was a virtue. German society accepted Alex and Wenzel as individuals. Their close relationship, however, drew suspicion. Most youths and conservative Germans referred to a homosexual as *der Schwule* (a fag). I couldn't ask my ignorant sister and brother-in-law to educate me about such things, so I asked Max about homosexuality.

"Timo, people are very much alike and at the same time often very much different," he explained with his strong hands on my shoulders which always preceded his fatherly lectures. "We all want love and acceptance, but not everyone loves and accepts in the same way. In our culture and many others, we learn, at a very young age, that love between a man and a woman is acceptable, or what is called 'normal.' As we grow older, we see that some people love in other ways, such as a man loving another man, or a woman loving another woman. Accepting that there are other types of love other than what is considered 'normal' is not easy for everyone.

"But that's where the difference between growing up and maturing enters. Everyone grows up, but not everyone matures. People who only grow up only accept what is 'normal.' People who mature accept that there is more in life than just the 'normal.' Do you understand?"

I may have said, "Yes," but using my fingers as a comb told Max that my young mind needed more information.

"Alex and Wenzel are men, just like us, but the way they love is different. I and other mature people accept that fact and accept them as friends."

He turned away from me—his way of letting me digest his words and come to my own conclusions.

It was early afternoon when we returned to Max's. Not knowing when the border guards were due to drive down the street, we left the wood in the truck and entered through the front door. Dora sat by the security light switch, and Helga worked in the kitchen.

"They came by about fifteen minutes ago. They're due back soon," said Doris, so we waited for their next round.

When she saw the military van in front of where the Beckers once lived, she flicked the switch once. The vehicle passed by Max's house, and as the taillights rounded the corner down the block, she flicked the switch twice.

The men in the chicken coop must have resumed work, and we unloaded the wood. Max had let his two dozen chickens roam within his fenced-in yard as he usually did during the day. They parted as we walked through them, and Alex knocked (three short knocks, a pause, and two more—our agreed signal) on the door. Max had fixed the latch lock, so it could be opened or closed from both sides of the door.

"It's about time you lazy bums showed up," said Gerhard who leaned on his pickax near the hole.

All five men were shirtless, and their skin shimmered with sweat. Ralf emerged up a ladder from the pit. They had dug three meters deep with only one meter left to our planned depth.

"Let's show these weak old men how to finish this job," Alex said to me.

He and I stacked the lumber in the corner and took off our shirts, but before we could grab a pickax and shovel, everyone froze.

The security light in the corner flashed three times.

Someone was coming.

Chapter 24

Max stepped up onto a shelf of hen nests and peeked through a thin crack in the wall. The wooden backyard fence gate creaked.

"It's just my neighbor," said Max as he jumped down and exited. He opened and closed the door behind him as if there were chickens inside and he didn't want them to escape. "Frau Schafhauser, what—"

He interrupted his own question when he saw the problem. The older couple's new German shepherd puppy had crawled under the fence and into the yard.

Max scooped up the dog and said, "Looks like your dog wants to meet my chickens."

The woman's frown turned to a wide smile when she saw that Max wasn't angry. She wore no makeup, jewelry, or a fancy hairdo, but she didn't need any of that. She was a natural beauty.

She flicked her long brown hair over her shoulder and said, "I am so sorry, Herr Thomas. Bach is our new baby *Hund*, and his curiosity gets him into trouble. He must have dug his way like a rabbit under your fence."

Reminded of the prior rabbit incident, Max smiled at the irony, handed her the puppy, and said, "No problem, but for my chicken's sake, better keep him closer to home."

"*Danke*," she said and left with her dog.

Max reentered the coop, and we all sighed with relief.

We reached our goal of creating a hole four meters deep and a meter square within the next hour and a half. Helga and Dora had prepared a filling meal of poached cod fish in a mustard sauce (most Christian Germans observed the tradition of avoiding eating meat on Good Friday) and potatoes. I excused myself before dessert, so I could meet Martina at the library and walk her home from work.

Even though I was ten minutes early to the end of Martina's shift, she was sitting on the library steps and reading.

"What are you doing out here?" I asked.

"I just got fired."

"What? I thought you were quitting."

"I was," Martina explained. "But when I gave Hilda (the Nazi-like head librarian who hated me) my one-week advance notice a few minutes ago, she said, 'Well, you might as well go right now if that's what you think of this position.' So, here I am."

I looked through the glass door.

Her former boss appeared agitated as she spoke to another employee. She made emphatic gestures and pointed at Martina standing on the steps.

"Well," I said, "It looks like Hilda is taking it well."

When Martina turned and saw Hilda's frantic state, she laughed and said, "Come on. Let's get out of here."

We walked hand-in-hand down the main street and toward the forest path. As soon as we entered the woods, Martina threw her arms around my neck and gave me a passionate kiss.

"Let's sit on the bench for a moment. We need to talk," she said.

We sat in silence for a few minutes. Martina stared at her hands folded in her lap as if she was recalling a memorized speech.

"I need to ask a few things of you," she said. "First, I've made an appointment with a doctor in Schönholz for Monday morning. I need to know for sure if I am pregnant or not. Can you take time off work and go with me?"

"Of course," I said and put my arm around her.

She directed her words toward me but focused on her fidgeting hands.

"Are you busy on Sunday?"

"No."

Max never worked on Sundays, especially Easter Sunday.

"Can you ask Max if you can borrow one of his trucks on Sunday? I plan on moving into my friend Greta's apartment on that day."

"On Easter?"

Martina's parents still paid reverence to Christian holidays, but she and her brother did not.

"Yes, Greta will be with her parents in Potsdam on Easter, so we won't be disturbing her. I don't have that much to move, but if we use a truck, we can do it in one trip."

"I'll ask him, but I don't see a problem."

I did foresee a problem. We would start dispersing soil from the tunnel on Saturday. The bottom of the trailer would be filthy. I would either have to wash it thoroughly or use the open bed trailer. That would be fine … if it didn't rain.

We continued strolling through the woods. It hit me all at once. In less than a month, my life would change and never be the same. I might be an expectant father living with his wife in his own house and running his own business or a free man living in West Germany or anywhere I wanted. I vowed not to be Timo, a teenager living in a dingy apartment with his disgusting sister and brother-in-law, working in East Germany at a menial job, and being a slave to communism.

I got to work an hour early the next day before any of the others had arrived and wasted no time asking Max for Monday off and the use of a truck on Sunday.

"Sure, Timo, I have no plans for Easter Sunday but to go to church, relax, and have dinner with Sven and Dora. Either truck is yours. As for Monday, Sven and Alex can handle delivering the dirt and picking up more lumber."

I thanked him but hadn't mentioned the reason for my asking for time off.

Max must have sensed that I was hiding something and asked, "Is there something else on your mind?"

"Yes, Max. Martina might be pregnant. If she is, I'll be staying and would like to take you up on the offer of your house and business, if the offer still stands. Whether she is, or she isn't, I'll work like a slave building this tunnel and let you know if I'll be leaving or not whenever I decide … It might not be until the day of the escape."

He looked at me as if he had seen me for the first time and said, "Timo, you haven't just grown up. You have also matured."

I couldn't have felt prouder if I had received a gold medal at the Olympics.

"Now," he said more like Max-the-boss, "I have a special job for you and Sven today. We have enough support lumber for the next two days, so I'll need Alex here directing the work as we start building the tunnel toward the wall. You and Sven will deliver the dirt we dug out yesterday to Magda's daycare center."

The others arrived, and our daily routine began. After I burned that day's plan sheet, we broke up into our work stations. Helga and Dora felt comfortable doing, as Sven termed it, "cooking and looking" duties in the house. Sven, Max, and I loaded the truck with pails of dirt. The rest of the men worked in the henhouse building the tunnel.

After loading the dirt, Max said to Sven and me, "Take about ten or twelve chickens and a few buckets of feed with you. The kids will get a kick out of taking care of them."

Nothing makes men look more like idiots than chasing chickens, but that's what Sven and I did for the next ten minutes.

Magda must have alerted the children that the chickens and their farmland were coming that day because they all cheered when they saw our truck. It was Saturday, and the daycare operated six days per week since most parents worked every day but Sunday.

The property behind the one-story building had a swing set, slide, seesaw, and sandbox close to the main facility. A vacant lot extended far beyond the playground for about fifty meters more than a soccer field. A rusting cyclone fence surrounded the entire property. At the back of the lot and far from the main building, an old woodshed stood which made a perfect makeshift chicken coop.

I backed up the truck to the fence. We opened the trailer doors and dropped the chickens into the yard. The children screamed—some with delight and others with fear, but they seemed to be enjoying the experience. As the chickens and children chased each other, Sven handed me buckets of fresh soil that I spread over the tilled terrain.

When we finished, Magda gathered the kids together, and they sang a song that they had rehearsed as a thank-you to Herr Thomas. Sven rewarded them with corny jokes and magic tricks like pulling coins out of their ears.

Anxiety built inside me as I watched them, mesmerized by Sven's antics. In less than forty-eight hours my fate would be determined.

Chapter 25

Easter Sunday, April 22, 10:20 a.m.

Max was still at church when I picked up the flatbed truck. The weather forecast called for sunny skies, gradual clouding, and a chance for thundershowers by late afternoon. I took the chance that we would not need the covered trailer, since Schönholz was only a twenty-minute drive from Glienicke/Nordbahn, and Martina and I could load and unload her belongings before the threat of rain. Besides, I was too lazy to sweep out the dirt and chicken droppings from Saturday.

When I arrived at Martina's, I began to doubt my choice of trailers. She only had four boxes filled with clothes, shoes, and personal belongings, but I hadn't anticipated her entire bedroom set, including two dressers, two nightstands, lamps, and her bed.

"Do we have time to utilize your bed one last time before you move?" I asked.

"Don't be silly. My parents will be home from church soon. Anyway, that's what created our current problem."

I laughed at what I thought was a joke, but she wasn't even smiling as she finished packing a box full of underwear. While she finished packing, I wandered into the kitchen and spotted a pamphlet on the table. The cover illustration was a black, red, and gold striped shield with a bow compass and hammer in the center. The shield rested on a sword with the blade and the black handle exposed. The words, *Shield and Sword of the Party*, the Stasi motto in bold black letters, headlined the title page.

"What is this?" I said like a parent who had just discovered stolen property in his child's room.

Martina ran into the kitchen and had a startled expression when she saw me holding the pamphlet. After a few seconds, she put a hand to her chest and exhaled before speaking.

"Oh, you scared me, Timo. I thought you saw a rat or something. That? I don't know, just some propaganda Olaf brought home yesterday. I think Christian gave it to him. His brother works for the Stasi, I think."

I tossed it back onto the table and thought, *don't I know his brother works for the Stasi.*

We used the hand truck and the dolly I had brought to load her furniture and left before noon. Traveling on Karl-Liebknecht-Straße took us past the park where we had spent the summer swimming in Kindel Lake. I wondered if we would ever return. If so, I further pondered if we could ever enjoy it the way we had in the past.

I doubted it. It's difficult to explain. The lake was our playground of innocence. We teased, laughed, and played with no recognition that our love grew, and we matured with every passing warm summer hour. Losing our virginity in the lake that day had changed everything. Physically, we can go back there, but our playground somehow had changed.

"How are you feeling?" I asked.

"Terrible."

She stared out her window and didn't look at the park entrance.

"Is it … what do they call it, morning sickness?"

"No, I'm just worried about going to the doctor's office tomorrow."

We sat in silence as I turned onto B96a, the main highway to Schönholz. The silence continued as we traveled down the residential streets. For some reason, I felt like we were fugitives, guilty of a shameful crime.

Martina spoke when the highway cut into the rural region.

"How do you feel about it?"

"If you are pregnant, we'll marry," I said and stared straight ahead at the road.

"And what?" Martina now glared at me. "Live off your meager earnings? And where are we supposed to live?"

I couldn't answer her without talking about the tunnel, so I just said, "I have bigger plans than that."

"Plans? What plans?" She asked and turned her whole body toward me. "And how do you know what I want?"

"What do you want?"

She folded her arms in front of her, turned away from me, and fixated straight ahead through the windshield before answering.

"I don't know."

"Are you thinking of an abortion?"

I looked at her and almost drove into the oncoming lane.

"Yes. I mean no ... I don't know. I'm so confused, no matter how much I think about it."

She leaned toward me, and I put my arm around her.

"Timo, help me. Don't leave me now," she said and closed her eyes.

The road took us through a wooded area with tall green trees and a running stream visible from the highway. The natural beauty produced a tranquilizing mood that calmed both of us.

The actual town of Schönholz, where Martina went to school, was even smaller and quainter than Glienicke/Nordbahn. Her apartment complex stood in the area just south of it known as Berlin-Schönholz, more bustling and metropolitan.

"That's the building there," Martina said and pointed to a five-story structure on the main street.

"Please tell me you live on the first or second floor," I said and thought of all the bedroom furniture in the back.

She put on her mischievous little girl smile, cocked her head, and said, "*Nein*, it's on the fifth floor."

I didn't even bother to ask if there was an elevator. This monstrosity of an apartment development reminded me of my residence. The Soviets built hundreds of these huge, ugly, cheap structures to house its East German working class, and at the end of each building a winding, steep, cold, metal staircase led dwellers to their floor, but with no elevator.

We parked near the east entrance and left her belongings in the truck. She wanted to show me the apartment first. The clouds foreshadowing the predicted afternoon thunderstorm had started to form. My job as a hauler had prepared my body for climbing and carrying, but this steep staircase shortened my breath and made me sweat by the time we reached the fifth-floor.

Martina fumbled with her keys. Her new apartment was the first one next to the stairwell. My head shook at the sight of the sterile, vacant, uncarpeted hallway and the hollow, metal flight of stairs. Every noise would echo and amplify throughout the staircase and corridor and penetrate through the cheap apartment door.

I had expected that we would have been the only two movers, but when she walked in ahead of me, she said, "Oh, I didn't expect that you'd be here already."

I almost ran out when I saw the two people sitting on the couch and watching TV.

"Your roommate was just leaving when we got here," said Olaf, "so she let us in and said we could wait. Christian was off duty until tonight, too, so I asked him—"

"No," interrupted Christian, "the truth is I volunteered. I wanted to help Martina move, and when I heard you would be with her, Timo,

I wanted to talk to you. Olaf and Martina, why don't both of you go down and start unloading? We'll join you in a minute. I want to talk with Timo."

They both left. I could tell by Martina's expression that she was as surprised as I to see Christian. She started to apologize, but Olaf escorted her out.

My body tensed with anger at the sound of the closing door. I wanted to kill him just as he had killed Hannah. No, I wanted him to suffer first. The last time we met at Christmas, I chose flight. This time I would choose fight, but something held me back. It wasn't fear. It was the look on his face and his tone. He looked like a helpless puppy, and his voice quivered as he spoke.

"I know you must hate me for what—"

"Hate you? I more than hate you. I want to kill you, and how would you know how—"

"Because I hated myself, too."

He sat at the small kitchen table and buried his face in his hands. When he removed them, tears had streaked down his face.

Softened, but not fully convinced of his remorse, I sat opposite him and listened.

"I won't bore you with the standard 'I was only doing my job' excuse. I knew the moment my commander ordered me to shoot her that it wasn't in me to be a border guard or any type of military person. No one, not even Olaf, just one other person and you, know this—I was going to quit, maybe even desert or escape."

"Why didn't you?" I asked and found myself leaning over the table as if I were interrogating him.

"A guard on my shift, the other person I shared my thoughts with, talked me out of it. He said that he had the same doubts about being a border guard and so did many other guards. He said, 'I don't know if I could kill a fellow German. I'm not an East or West German, just a

German. Let's give border guard duty another chance.' Anyway, it's all I have. My parents were killed in the war. I live with my older brother in Potsdam. He's … a state official."

I sat back in my chair and my attention on him turned to introspection. I wondered how much Christian knew. He had recommended me to his brother for recruitment in the National People's Army.

Did he know that his brother had acted on his recommendation? Did he know I gave the names of those defectors at that factory? He talked as if he didn't. My instincts told me not to ask and to let him continue.

"My education was a dead end. My marks weren't high enough in polytechnic secondary school for anything but building trades, which I hate. My brother used his influence and got me enrolled in training for border guard duty."

Hearing that his parents were killed in the war and that he lived with a sibling created empathy and perhaps sympathy within me. He was a prisoner of circumstance, just like me. Within his limits of choice, he picked the life of a soldier, and I elected that of an independent laborer. I started to share these thoughts when we were interrupted by Martina's voice reverberating up the stairwell walls.

"*Dummkopf.*"

We rushed out and stood at the top of the stairs.

Olaf had one hand on the railing and the other clutching the flap of the half-empty cardboard box Martina had been packing earlier when I was in the kitchen. He was regaining his balance after tripping up the stairs. Martina stood on the landing of the fourth floor and looked at her bras and panties littered on the stairs and railings below. All of us, excluding Olaf who expressed the look of a kid who got caught cheating in class, laughed at the once sterile stairwell now decorated with women's underwear.

The move took less than an hour with four young bodies working.

"I thought military men were supposed to be in shape," I teased when Olaf and Christian collapsed onto the sofa after hauling a heavy dresser with an attached mirror up the stairs.

"Don't worry," said Olaf between gasps. "When we get you into the border guards, you'll lose all that physical strength of a hauler."

I just smiled and felt relief that the move was done and the tension between Christian and me had been lifted.

Olaf and Christian left to get some rest before working their night-shift guard duties.

Martina didn't talk much during the move and remained aloof after they left.

"What's wrong?" I asked.

"I'm just worried about tomorrow."

I cuddled her, and she wept as if she didn't want anyone to hear. We watched television and ate the sausages, bread, and potato salad I had bought at a food stand down the block. We were all alone, but I knew Martina was not in the mood to make love, so I just stayed with her until early evening.

The following morning, we met at the government medical center just a few blocks away. It looked more like a traffic court room than a clinical waiting room. Cheap plastic chairs lined the barren, dirty, white walls. Rows of more chairs faced a single wooden desk where a military man sat with stacks of forms and an open ledger-type book. Young women with babies, old men with canes, and every age and class of Germans in between occupied all but a dozen seats. A sign at the door with an arrow pointing to the desk read: REGISTRATION.

I secured two empty seats, and Martina approached the desk. After a brief mumbled exchange of words, the soldier checked his appointment ledger and handed her a card from one of his stacks and a pencil. She filled out a few lines, returned the card, and took a two-digit plastic-coated number from the desk.

We waited for three-and-a-half hours. Every so often, a fat, limping nurse emerged from the corridor behind the reception desk and read a number and a name from a card.

"Number 38, Martina ... Schmitke ... no, Schmitz ... no, Schmidt," said the nurse.

I had to nudge Martina because she had fallen asleep on my shoulder. I braced myself for another long wait, but she returned from the hallway of examining rooms within twenty minutes. I couldn't read the expression on her face. She headed straight for the exit, and I followed.

Outside, she stood with her head down as if she had been caught stealing.

I placed my finger under her chin and lifted her head, so our eyes met. She looked both sad and frightened.

"Well," I asked, "are we going to be parents?"

My question somehow seemed to relieve her stress.

"No, we are not."

"But there's more. I can tell. What else?'

She dropped her head again and kept walking.

Chapter 26

Saturday, April 28, 12:40 p.m.

"Wipe your shoes before coming in," said Helga to the men as they approached the back door after working in the chicken coop.

Alex and I had just returned from gathering support timber for the tunnel, and it was lunchtime.

"Why are your feet and clothes so muddy?" asked Dora.

"We ran into some wet soil," said Max.

"Oh?" asked Alex. His eyes widened.

"Don't worry," said Wenzel as he took off his dirty shoes. "We're right below the barbed wire fence now. We figured that water from last week's rain has seeped down one of the post holes above us."

But the worried look didn't leave Alex's face throughout lunch.

Martina and I hadn't spoken since Monday when we left the doctor's office. Every time I called, Greta said she was in class, on an errand, or at work. She had a new part-time job working in the back room of the East Berlin Post Office. It was impossible for me to visit her at work the way I had when she worked at the library.

As my contact with Martina declined, the tunnel project progressed. Alex transformed an old wheel barrel into a pushcart on a rail to transport dirt through the tunnel and out the entrance shaft with a pulley system. We had dug eleven meters toward the wall. Our mission was on schedule with no major problems … until today.

After lunch, Alex and I led the other men through the tunnel. It was our turn to dig while the others either extracted dirt or built the overhead supports. With each step, our shoes became more and more caked and heavy with mud. By the time we reached our digging point, our feet were ankle deep in water. Above us, water seeped through the ceiling boards and plopped into deepening puddles.

"Oh, my God," said Alex. "I was afraid of this."

"What is it?" asked Max.

"I've seen this before. This isn't rain water. This is a water main leak. They probably damaged the mainline when they sunk the dead zone posts."

Gerhard and Ralf gaped at the wet ceiling as if trying to visualize the cracked water main above.

Wenzel hyperventilated.

"It's probably only a meter or so above us. Can't we dig toward it and fix it?" asked Gerhard.

"Only the East Berlin government has the means and equipment to fix it, and if we notify them, they'll surely discover our tunnel," said Alex.

"What'll we do?" asked Ralf.

"I don't know," answered Alex, "But if I'm right, our tunnel will be flooded out within forty-eight hours."

"We're doomed. I'm going to be sick. I hope I make it to your toilet, Max," Wenzel said, then gagged, ran toward the entrance shaft, and scurried up the ladder.

Alex sloshed in the ankle-deep water and rubbed his chin. A slight grin developed as he spoke.

"Wenzel's words have given me an idea." He took measured steps back to the deepening puddle where water from the support roof dripped into it like rain. "We're practically under the dead zone here. Am I right?"

The others nodded.

"That means our former main road into Berlin is directly above us. That also means that, although the water main located two meters below the street is above us, the main sewer line should be less than two meters either directly below us or within a meter or less toward the wall.

"Timo, remember the construction site near Alexanderplatz we visited last Saturday?"

"Yes."

"Go there and tell the foreman I need a two, no make it a three-meter drainpipe. Tell him I'm putting it in my basement and connecting it to the sewer line. Hurry." He looked at his watch. "It's Saturday, and they stop working soon. The rest of you grab shovels and start digging in the puddle at a slight angle toward the wall. If we're lucky, we'll hit the city's main storm-sewage line within a few meters."

"What if we don't?" asked Gerhard.

"Like Wenzel said, we're doomed."

The construction crew had just quit when I got to the site. The foreman growled at my request but ordered some workers to search the plumbing materials for the pipe and to load it onto the flatbed truck.

By the time I had gotten back to the tunnel, Ralf was almost waist deep in water as he dug in the almost two-meter-deep hole. The others, soaked and sodden with mud, watched and waited for their turn to dig.

"I'll need some help unloading that drainpipe. It's heavy."

No one responded. They all focused with sullen faces on the hole as Ralf dug.

Max looked at me and said, "We may not even need it, Timo. We're almost two meters deep and no—"

"I've hit something," said Ralf.

He shoveled some more mud, then raised the spade over his head and brought it down hard. Even through the water, we could hear the clang as the blade hit the cement surface of what had to be the man-sized sewer pipe.

"Hand me a pickax," said Ralf.

Three swings from Ralf's meaty arms and shoulders couldn't crack the pipe's surface.

"The water is too deep. It's slowing the momentum of the ax," said Alex.

"Damn it!" Ralf said and took one vehement swing with the pickax.

The water couldn't muffle the crunching sound as the pointed end of the ax penetrated the pipe. When Ralf pulled the pick ax from the crack, water swirled from the pit and disappeared into a small hole in the sewer wall.

The stench of sewer gas permeated the already dank smell throughout the tunnel. To us, it signaled success and couldn't have been more welcomed than a field of lilacs in a spring breeze until Alex yelled, "Put out that cigarette, Sven, that gas could explode any second!"

Sven stamped out his cigarette. He and I ran to get the drainpipe while Max and Alex chipped at the crack to widen it. By the time we fit the pipe into the hole, set the proper height to the tunnel floor, and refilled the pit around it, Saturday night had elapsed into early Sunday morning.

"We've conquered a major obstacle," said Max with a smile.

"The first of many, I predict," Alex said and stamped the loose dirt around the drainpipe opening.

Chapter 27

Sunday, April 29, 2:30 p.m.

"Is he going to sleep all fucking day?"

Horst's raspy smoker's voice awakened me, but I kept my eyes closed. No sense prolonging his half-drunken insults with my responses. He and Frieda would be leaving soon for their Sunday let's-try-to-be-a-normal-couple outing that would end in both becoming drunk and hostile.

"Let him sleep," said Frieda. "He worked late last night."

"Work, my *arsch*. He was probably out all night screwing his little girlfriend."

As soon as I heard them leave, I stood, stretched, and made some coffee. The Sunday edition of *Neues Deutschland* lay scattered on the kitchen table. I sat down and picked up the front page. The headline read: ANOTHER FAILED ESCAPE ATTEMPT:

> *19-year-old Horst Frank tried to "break through" to West Berlin at around half past midnight. According to a border police report, he had "already climbed over the wire fence when our guards called out to him. Since Frank continued his flight, our guards fired seven shots at him. F[rank] was transported to the People's Police Hospital where he died at approx. 4 a.m."*

Horst Frank marks the 19th death, shot at the "Schönholz" garden settlement at the sector border between Berlin-Pankow and Berlin-Reinickendorf.

The *Neues Deutschland* article didn't eulogize Horst Frank. The primary purpose of the short article followed by a long, itemized death list was to deter escape attempts through fear. It was working with me. The mention of "*Schönholz*" reminded me of my mission for that day—to find and to confront Martina about her avoidance of me.

Music played loud enough from Martina's apartment to be heard in the hallway, even with the metal door shut. I knocked hard enough to penetrate the rock and roll music. The music stopped, and seconds later the door opened. I readied myself to force it open if Martina tried to shut it, but her roommate answered.

"Yes?" she said.

"I'm Timo. I've come to see Martina."

"I'm Greta," she said.

"I came to see Martina."

"She went to the movies in East Berlin."

"What movie, and when did she leave?"

"I don't know which movie, but she left about an hour ago."

"That means she went to a late afternoon matinee. There aren't that many theaters in East Berlin. I'll find her," I said, turned, and headed for the door.

"Wait. I don't think you want to do that. You see, she's not alone. She's on a date."

Chapter 28

Tuesday, May 1, 12:10 p.m.

The others stood in line and waited to climb the ladder, exit the tunnel, and enter the house for lunch. I hung back and watched Wenzel's frail frame labor up the steps.

It had been almost two full days since I had left Martina's apartment. The thought of losing her to someone else obsessed me. I carried a bucket to the far end of the tunnel, now directly below the middle of the dead zone, that area between the barbed wire fence and the wall, turned over the pail, and sat on it. The silent eeriness of the dark and tall passageway provided a perfect sanctuary for a man to think, and I needed a time and a place to sort things out.

It was May Day, International Workers Day, a revered holiday in Germany and even more so by the Soviets. During World War II, the Nazis embraced the day and turned it into a political and military show of might with a long parade. After the war, the Allied countries divided Germany into four sectors and agreed that there would be no public parading of military strength, but every May Day the Soviets and East German government defied the agreement with a long procession of tanks, soldiers, and weaponry through the East Berlin streets.

No one worked that day. Everyone was expected to attend the parade.

We ignored the no work order in the morning but agreed to attend the parade after lunch. Since construction sites were closed, Alex and I couldn't gather lumber, and we would attract too much attention dumping dirt at the daycare center on May Day. So, we worked with the others in the tunnel.

Only two faint sounds disturbed the loneliness of my thoughts: the steady drip from the roof to the drain and indistinct murmuring from above. Now that we were below the dead zone, occasional conversations between the guards seeped through the ground above us. Their latest tactic for detecting tunnels was the use of listening devices on the surface, so we had to work in silence.

Every time I closed my eyes, I saw Martina. Sometimes she was laughing, other times weeping on my shoulder, and more often she was making love—those images hurt the most, because she made love with a faceless person, not me.

But two days of mourning and self-pity were enough. I had to face reality. If Martina was gone, then nothing held me in Glienicke/Nordbahn, East Berlin, or all of East Germany. I'd escape with the others and start a new life in West Berlin, West Germany, or maybe even another country like the USA. If I were to make such a dynamic life change, I needed to be positive that Martina and I were finished. How could I be sure if she wouldn't face me?

This time when I closed my eyes, I saw her working at her new job at the East Berlin post office. That's what gave me an idea.

"Timo, come eat. Your lunch is getting cold." Helga's whispering voice echoed from the opened hatch and throughout the tunnel.

"Coming," I said in my softest resounding tone.

My enlightened idea sparked my appetite which had been lost since Sunday, and I hurried through the tunnel as I thought about one of Helga's filling lunches.

The others had half-eaten their lunches when I sat down. Helga brought out a plate of bockwurst, knackwurst, sauerkraut, and potato salad she had kept warm in the oven for me.

"Eat the bockwurst first, Timo. It will make your *schwanz* grow," said Sven.

Dora gave him a punch on the arm, and everyone laughed.

I didn't care. Accepting their teasing was part of being the youngster. Anyway, my recent plan for resolving my relationship with Martina had kindled my appetite. I ate like a ravenous wolf.

Helga and Dora excused themselves and left for the kitchen to serve dessert.

"*Mein Gott!*" both screamed from the kitchen, and we all ran to join them.

We watched through the window as if we were seeing a television drama … but this was real. Frau Schafhauser, the neighbor with the puppy, stood with her arms crossed and stared at the opened door of the chicken coop. Her husband emerged from inside holding the German shepherd pup in his arms. The man's light-colored pants had dirt marks from the ladder steps, but it was his facial expression that told us he had discovered the tunnel. Herr Schafhauser, a rail ticket agent with grey/brown hair and of medium height and weight, looked as if he had witnessed a murder. He grabbed his wife's arm and escorted her out the gate.

Our previous laughter and loud conversation must have drowned the sound of squawking chickens when the dog entered the yard.

"Who left the door open?" said Gerhard.

It was more of an indictment than a question, and they all looked at me.

The little boy inside me wanted to run, hide, and cry, but that little boy had become more and more of a distant memory to me.

"It must have been me," I said.

"You idiot," said Gerhard. "How could you be so stupid?"

Wenzel ran toward me like a crazed child. "They're probably calling the authorities right now. We're doomed."

Alex grabbed and held him.

The others either grumbled or retreated into grave introspection.

From behind, two heavy hands rested on my shoulders. At first, I thought it was Max, but he was seated at the kitchen table. Ralf, the "Gentle Giant" who rarely spoke up, said, "Stop blaming Timo, all of you. How many times has one of us left that chicken coop unsecured when we broke for lunch?"

"He's right," Alex said. "It could have been any of us. We don't even know for sure if they discovered the tunnel."

"They saw it," Gerhard said and joined Max at the table. "Didn't you see the dirt on his pants and the look on his face? This reminds me of that scene in *The Diary of Anne Frank*."

"What are you talking about?" asked Helga.

The book about the Jewish family hiding from Nazis in the attic of a small business building in Amsterdam became popular when a German translation appeared in East German bookstores in 1957. Most literate East Germans had either read the book or seen the play in East Berlin.

"I'm talking about that scene after a burglar discovers the Jews hiding in the building. They worried about the possibility of the burglar turning them in to the Nazis."

"Yes," Wenzel said with his fists clenched and panic growing in his words, "and if I remember correctly, it led to their doom."

"You're forgetting a major difference, Wenzel," Max said as he stood and took center stage of the discussion. "In the Anne Frank story, the betrayer was a burglar, a stranger. These people are my neighbors."

"What's the difference?" asked Sven who held a frightened Dora in his arms.

"The difference my good friend, Sven, is the solution. I'm going to pay them a visit right now and find out what they know and what, if anything, they plan to do."

But it may have been too late … someone knocked at the door.

Wenzel raced upstairs to hide when Max approached the door.

"Maybe the rest of you should follow him," Max turned and said, but all stood their ground. If it was the military, border police, the Stasi, or whoever they sent to arrest traitors, we would go down together.

He opened the door.

"May we speak with you, Herr Thomas?" said a man's voice.

"Yes, come in."

Frau and Herr Schafhauser stepped inside. Frau, dressed in her usual tight-fitting housedress, held their little dog and stroked his head. When she saw all of us, she backed up toward the door, but Max touched her arm and reassured her.

"It's okay," he said. "They're friends of mine. Let's go into the kitchen and talk."

Herr Schafhauser had changed from his dirty pants to clean khaki trousers and wore a dark windbreaker. He also wore a tight, frightened expression as he nodded to each of us and followed Max who closed the kitchen door behind them.

We sat or stood in silence in the dining room and tried to listen to them talking, but we couldn't decipher the words. After about fifteen minutes, the back door opened and closed, and Max entered the dining room.

"Yes, they know about the tunnel, and they have agreed not to tell anyone."

Everyone sighed, but a general feeling of suspicion still lingered until Max spoke again.

"But only under one condition—they, including their dog, want to escape with us. I told them, 'yes,' but they would be last in line."

"I want to be last," said Helga. "I don't want my big body to hold anyone up."

Sven, instead of teasing her as he often did, put his arm around her and said, "Actually, Helga, Max and I agreed long ago that we would see that everyone escaped safely, so we would be last."

"We can decide who is first and last later," said Max. "My question to you—did I speak for everyone when I promised them a place in line?"

All but Gerhard and Magda gave their approval. Magda, now more at ease speaking in front of the group, said, "Max ... I like dogs as much as anyone ... but ..."

"But what if the animal barks or does something to give us away?" Gerhard finished her thought.

"That's why I put them last in line, Gerhard, but the most import-ant question we have is obvious—do we really have any choice but to allow them and their dog a place?"

"You're right," Gerhard said.

Magda and the rest of us agreed.

"Wenzel, you mouse, come down here. It's all over." Alex yelled up the stairs.

Wenzel crept down the stairs as if each step might be his last.

"What's going on?" he asked.

Sven met him at the bottom of the stairwell, put his arm around him, and said in a hushed voice, "It was the border guards. They said neighbors thought Max might be building a tunnel in back. We told them we knew nothing about it, but a suspicious little man was hiding upstairs who had been doing something in the chicken coop the past week. They're waiting to speak to you out front."

"Don't even joke like that," Wenzel said, ran to the front window, and looked out.

"You inconsiderate idiots," Helga said and left through the front door.

"Where are you going?" asked Dora, but Helga had shut the door before answering.

"I know my wife," said Ralf with assurance. "She's just going across the road and inviting the Schafhausers for dessert."

I tried to leave unnoticed, but Alex saw that I had grabbed my windbreaker and asked, "Are you leaving before dessert again, Timo?"

"Yes, but I may see all of you at the parade this afternoon," I lied, because I had something much more important to do than watch a silly military pageant.

I zipped up my jacket and left.

Chapter 29

Thousands of people gathered behind the ropes separating them from East Berlin's main street to watch the May Day parade. Max and his friends stood in the back to watch, or in Max's words, "to tolerate the spectacle." For children and young sympathizers of the "Soviet state of mind," the five-hour parade symbolized unity, pride, and military might, but it reminded older people of destruction and despair. The procession followed the same route that the Soviet army had used in April of 1945 when they marched into Berlin and literally raped and pillaged along the way.

Max, Sven, Dora, and Alex sipped their beers purchased from one of the strolling vendors weaving through the crowds. Behind them, Wenzel rocked from side to side with some drunken cronies. Farther down the street and closer to the grandstand, Soviet Premier Khrushchev and state and party leadership viewed the pageant.

Several military men goose-stepped down the middle of the street with a billboard sized banner displaying the words: LONG LIVE THE 1ST OF MAY. The National People's Army band made up of private citizens, neighbors who volunteered to help the Stasi and promote the Soviet way of life, followed in their flared, gun-colored helmets and brown, tapered uniforms with matching leather gloves and boots. They looked less like German citizens and more like Nazi soldiers. We held our ears as the horn section blasted a Soviet anthem.

The last booming National People's Army drum faded down the street, and the spectators waited for the next martial display. A drunken man with his arm around Wenzel mumbled, "I wish this was the last May Day parade I had to drink through."

"*Hallo*, my friends. This *is* my last parade. I'm leaving!" Wenzel said as if announcing a fire.

Alex, Max, Dora, and Sven exchanged astonished expressions.

"What do you mean by that?" asked the man as he squeezed Wenzel tighter.

"What he means," said Sven who turned, removed the man's arm from Wenzel's shoulders, and replaced it with his own, "is that he's had enough to drink, and he's leaving with his friend, Alex."

Alex nodded and proceeded to take charge of Wenzel. He moved Sven aside and ducked under Wenzel's arm.

"Either that," Sven continued with a wry smile, "or he means he's leaving with Khrushchev back to Moscow to carry the Premiere's shit pail."

As everyone in earshot laughed, Alex tried to prop up Wenzel who collapsed to the pavement like a bag of sand.

Only an elderly couple and I boarded the bus at the Glienicke/ Nordbahn stop. It was late afternoon, and the May Day parade had started hours ago.

After leaving Max's, I had spent the afternoon in our apartment drafting a letter to Martina. The silence and solitude of the building reminded me of the peace of mind I had experienced earlier in the day. All the building residents, including Frieda and Horst, had left for the parade that morning. Of course, my sister and brother-in-law couldn't have given a damn about the event. Their interest was in drinking beer before, during, and after the celebration.

My mission was to hand deliver my letter to Martina. Knowing that she had probably attended the parade, I could at least slip it under her apartment door.

The couple sat in the front of the bus, and I took a seat toward the rear. Funny, they looked like an older version of Martina and me. Their weathered faces seemed painted into perpetual smiles. He looked older than she and wore a lightweight jacket and pleated trousers. She reminded me of Helga but with shorter hair and a quieter voice. They appeared to be on an adventurous date as they chatted with the driver about the unusual lack of traffic and the probable crowds and mayhem at the parade.

Because of the lack of passengers, the light bus amplified every bump and turn until I felt a little nauseated. I moved from my position, directly over a rear wheel, to a seat in the back. Out of boredom, I opened the envelope and proofread the letter for maybe the tenth time:

> *Dear Martina,*
>
> *I hope you are well. Please read this letter, since it may be the last time I reach out to you. I promise not to bother you again, if that's your wish.*
>
> *At first, I was angry at you. As the days have gone by, I realized more and more your reasons for ending our relationship. You want beautiful and expensive things. I'm content with simpler things. You want someone with high ambitions. I just want freedom. You want a university education. I do not. You accept and embrace what you and your brother call "the Soviet state of mind." I don't understand its meaning. You are moving on to a new life with new friends. I am in the same place.*

What confuses me is your method of telling me, by avoidance. Is that all I meant to you? Is that all we meant to each other? Have you forgotten our summer days at the lake? Our Sundays? Our gifts? Our deep conversations?

I would be lying if I said, "I don't love you anymore," because I still do. But I'd never beg you to come back if you didn't feel the same way. I just need to know from you, either face-to-face, by a letter, or, even if you must do so, through the words of your brother that we are through.

I need to know very, very soon.

Still in Love,

Timo

The bus came to a screeching halt at the Berlin-Schönholz bus stop. The couple and the driver stared at me as if I were an alien when I stepped off the bus. They must have thought it strange that a young person wouldn't be at the parade. I felt like a human on an alien planet because there was no sign of life. It reminded me of an episode of an American program, *The Twilight Zone*, broadcast from a West Berlin television station. A man found himself in a little town with everything but people. He'd wander around the streets and see signs of life: food cooking in a diner, a jukebox playing in a bar, even a movie theater with the marquee lights on and popcorn popping at the concession counter, but no people. He went completely crazy. In the end, he's an astronaut in training. He had been confined to an isolation room located within an aircraft hangar for almost 500 hours. They were testing his fitness for a spaceflight to the moon. He had hallucinated the whole concept of the town due to the strain.

I had been through a lot of "psychological stress" because of Martina, the tunnel, my home life, and more. I wondered if I was just hallucinating.

On my way, I passed the medical building and recalled the last day I saw Martina and her strange behavior when she told me the pregnancy exam results.

The only sounds in the apartment building were my footsteps on the metal stairs as I climbed to the fifth floor. After knocking on the door for several minutes, I slipped the letter under it.

Martina would answer my letter somehow. I knew her well enough to know that.

Chapter 30

Wednesday, May 2, 10:35 a.m.

Alex and I sat in the back of the truck trailer and watched the children work and play in their *Kinderbauernhof* (children's farm). We had spread buckets of dirt from yesterday's tunnel work, and Magda supervised small groups either raking, hoeing, planting or tending the chickens.

Alex hadn't talked much, but he was in happy spirits. "Too bad you missed the parade, Timo."

"Why? Anything different from the usual show of military might?"

"No, the parade was a typically long, dull event, but we were drunk enough to have a good time. I'm afraid my friend, Wenzel, had too great of a time. He was sick this morning and didn't want to come to work, but I told him he'd feel better later and brought him."

"Where are we going today to pick up lumber?" I asked.

"To Mönchmühle. They're rebuilding the old train station there, and I've worked with that contractor before. Oh, that reminds me. Helga wants us to stop at the bakery there and buy a cake. We're quietly celebrating tonight."

"What are we celebrating?"

"After you left yesterday, we realized two things. First, exactly one week from today, our tunnel should be completed, and we'll be leaving.

Second, by the end of our work today, we should be directly beneath the wall and ready to dig below the final dead zone."

Magda blew a whistle, and the children formed two lines.

The kids groaned and complained.

"Stop moaning," Magda said to the children. "We can work more on our farm tomorrow. Now let's march inside and wash up."

We passed the Glienicke/Nordbahn post office on our way to Mönchmühle. During our fifteen-minute ride, I thought about Martina working at her new job at the East Berlin post office. *Would she answer my letter by mail?* If she did, I wouldn't get it until early next week—not much time to decide whether to escape or stay. *Would she have Olaf talk to me?* That didn't sound like Martina. She loved her brother, but we shared the same opinion. He's a *Dummkopf.*

My hope was that we could soon discuss our relationship face-to-face.

Alex spent over an hour reminiscing with his old construction buddy in Mönchmühle, while I loaded the truck with wood. By the time we got to the bakery in town, it was past noon, and the bakery staff had left for lunch. I wanted to break for lunch, too, but Alex insisted that Helga and Dora would heat up food for us when we returned. In my opinion, he thought that if we got back late enough and took time to eat, we'd spend less time taking our turns digging in the tunnel.

We didn't get back to Max's house until almost three o'clock. I backed up the truck toward the chicken coop, and we entered the house to see when the last routine border patrol vehicle had passed.

The house was empty.

In the kitchen, some of the dishes and utensils soaked in cold water. I ran to the chicken coop. My knuckles tapped out our five-knock signal on the door. No one answered, so I unlatched it. The cement slab had been placed over the hole with the stove centered on top.

"Are they in there?" asked Alex standing at the back door.

"No, and everything is closed up."

"Check upstairs."

I hurried up the steps, inspected every room, and yelled, "Max? Anyone?" in a desperate attempt for a response.

"*Mein Gott*," said Alex when I reached the bottom stair. "You don't think ... You don't think they, the police, discovered our tunnel, do you? You don't think they were all arrested?"

He wasn't questioning either me or himself. Of course, that's what we thought. What else could it be? That's when I remembered Christian's brother. He had tried to recruit me again to spy on our Professor Gerhard Lehr, who they suspected of defecting. I had forgotten all about that because I had no intention of becoming an informer, but that didn't mean the Stasi hadn't been doing their own espionage. Maybe they had been following Gerhard and discovered the tunnel in the process. Maybe I should have told Max and the others about all this and excluded myself from helping with the tunnel.

I sat down at the dining room table and held my head in my hands. That's when I saw the note attached to the centerpiece. It looked as if someone frightened, hurried, or both had written it.

> *Alex,*
> *Go to Friedrichshain Municipal Hospital.*
> *Wenzel is very sick.*
> *Helga*

Alex insisted on driving his car, but I wouldn't let him. We took the truck, and I drove. I had never seen him so upset. Friedrichshain Municipal Hospital, located on the south end of East Berlin, was about an hour's ride from Max's house. He stared out the truck window and didn't speak except for the occasional remark, "I should have let him stay home."

I responded, "If you had, who would be there to take him to a hospital? We don't even know what's wrong," but that didn't appease him.

It didn't help Alex that since the mid-1950s, more than twenty-five per cent of the medical doctors in Berlin had fled to the West. The Soviets took over the hospitals and filled vacancies with poorly trained medical students and Russian doctors who cared little for Germans.

My feelings were mixed. I was concerned about Wenzel, but relieved that the tunnel hadn't been discovered and the others hadn't been arrested.

The hospital looked more like a government office building than a medical facility. The four-story structure stretched a half block long. Rows of dirty square windows lined each floor of the faded brown bricks barely held together with disintegrating mortar. Before I could complete maneuvering the truck into a parking space, Alex was inside the main entrance doors. By the time I entered, he was gone.

"Excuse me," I said to the nurse on duty at the front desk. "My friend, the man who was just here, where—"

"Elevator to the third floor," she said without looking up from writing in a log book of some kind.

On the third floor, elevator doors opened to chaotic activity. Medical staff in blue, green, or white uniforms and caps hustled between stations sectioned off by tall white-curtained room dividers. A few sickly-looking patients with oxygen masks lay on movable beds and waited for attention.

I didn't see anyone I recognized, so I moved to the left where I saw a door marked *Wartezimmer* (waiting room). Sven stood up among about a dozen people seated in plastic chairs and met me at the door.

"Come with me, Timo. There are some smaller conference rooms down the hall. Let's see if we can find an empty one."

As soon as we found one, he closed the door behind us and spoke.

"Wenzel had a heart attack in the tunnel."

I tried to talk, but he had anticipated all my questions.

"He's alive. We don't know the extent of it yet. Alex and Max are with him in one of those stations. He's in an oxygen tent and heavily sedated.

"We had been working hard all morning and just about reached where we thought the wall was directly above us. Wenzel didn't seem right, but we all thought it was because of all his drinking at the parade yesterday. Of course, we teased him about it, and he took it well enough, but I noticed something, not just in Wenzel, but in all of us. The deeper we got into the tunnel, the harder it was to breathe. Anyway, just before lunch, Wenzel looked particularly weak. We told him to break for lunch, and we'd join him soon."

He stopped talking when a thin doctor in black-rimmed glasses followed by a young couple stopped in the hallway just outside our door. When he saw us through the glass, he continued down the corridor. We heard the door in the conference room next to ours open and then close, and Sven continued talking, but lowered his voice.

"About a half hour later we found him lying at the base of the ladder. He must have collapsed while climbing up. I thought he was dead. His face was a ghostly white, and his hands were cold. Gerhard had had some brief medical training, and he performed some type of respiratory revival technique. Wenzel came around, but he was weak and could barely speak. We carried him into the house. Either Helga or Dora called an ambulance."

Within a few minutes, Max joined us in the room.

"Alex and the doctor are with him now."

"How bad is it?" asked Sven.

"The doctor is examining him now, but he won't know for sure until after they've done some tests. We have a big problem. In all his grogginess, Wenzel is mumbling. He's mentioned the tunnel a few times. I told Alex he must be with him at all times when he's awake."

Almost on cue, Alex entered.

"Don't worry. The doctor gave him a stronger sedative. He'll be sleeping deeply for hours and can't speak. I can tell you this. I won't be working on the tunnel anymore, and I won't leave East Berlin without him."

Chapter 31

Thursday, May 3, 9:30 a.m.

Glum. That was the only way to describe the group's mood at our morning meeting session before work.

Max studied the faces of us seated at the dining room table before speaking.

"I know how we all feel right now, but there are realities we need to face. We can't do anything for Wenzel but pray. We'll know more about his condition within the next twenty-four hours after they've done some tests."

"Is he conscious?" asked Dora who began filling empty coffee cups at the table.

"I talked with Alex this morning, and the doctors describe his state as 'stable.' They're keeping him heavily sedated. Alex will be with him constantly which brings us to our next concern. We've lost two workers."

"And our source of support lumber," added Ralf.

"Timo, how do stand with the wood supply?" asked Sven as he sipped his coffee.

"We picked up enough to get us through today and tomorrow. Alex said he would check for more construction sites on Friday."

"Good," said Max. "You'll have to do the dirt dumping at the children's center on your own and then get right back here. We'll need you in the tunnel, and we'll worry about getting more lumber tomorrow."

"We still have the problem of breathing," said Gerhard. "The air is getting thin down there."

"I have a solution for that," said Sven. "I'll show you when we get inside the chicken house."

"Anything else?" asked Max as he passed around the day's worksheet.

By now, there was no need to look at it. Each sheet for the past several days had looked the same. We knew how to build a tunnel. The only thing different from one day to the next, was the sketch of the ground above. That's what I liked to see, our tunnel beneath the first fence, then under the dead zone, and then beneath the wall itself. It showed our progress. When we finished today, we would have broken beneath the final dead zone on the other side of the wall.

After performing the ritual of igniting the worksheet and throwing it into the fireplace, I left to spread the soil.

During that ride to the daycare center, I experienced one of the strangest feelings in my life. Everything was perfect: the sky was cloudless and a tranquil blue; the sun warmed the dew on the bright green grass and my skin in the morning spring breeze; the trees, the leaves, plants, squirrels, every living thing seemed serene and in a natural harmony with its surroundings. My mind fixated in the moment—not the past, not the future, just now.

Although my experience with alcohol was limited, it wasn't like being drunk. I enjoyed the taste of beer when Max offered it, but dreaded the sluggish, full feeling from drinking too much. The previous July, Martina and I had joined another couple at Kindel Lake. The boy had brought a couple of marijuana cigarettes that he had somehow obtained from a cousin. I had never seen, let alone smoked one before, and felt nervous about the experience. Martina insisted that we try it. She had a way of getting me to do things by challenging my manhood. "Don't be a little girl," she'd say.

My fear was that I'd become delusional and do something dangerous, but that didn't happen. Instead, my senses heightened, and my surroundings came alive: the waves slapping against the shore, the summer wind whispering between the trees, the warm sun drawing the wetness from my skin, Martina strolling toward the water in her short-skirted swimsuit. In my young life, I had experienced tranquility and keen awareness, but never melded together into one sensation like that. Marijuana had affected me that way, and that's how I felt on May 3, 1962 while driving to the daycare center.

During the drive, this euphoric sensation gave way to a sobering sadness. Within a few days, I might be leaving forever, everything gone, forever. I would miss all of it: Martina, the lake, the town, my job, even my sister and disgusting brother-in-law and their drunkenness. My hands shook on the steering wheel, and my breathing shortened to quick gasps.

I pulled the truck to the side of the road and sat until the panic passed.

I had spread the soil on the children's farm and watched the kids work and play.

"How is Wenzel?" said a voice from behind me. It was Magda.

"The doctors say he is 'stable,' and they'll know more after some testing," I said to Magda who now stood next to me.

We watched the children in silence. Magda and I rarely spoke with each other. She was a shy woman and, like her husband, intelligent.

"Magda, are you scared?"

"Pardon me?"

"I mean about leaving ... your friends, your job, the kids ... your fellow workers here?"

When I mentioned her staff, her face tightened, and she focused on two boys arguing over feeding the chickens. "What have I told you two about fighting?" she said to them. "Share."

I interpreted her reaction as not wanting to answer, so I kept quiet, but she responded, "Yes, of course, I'm scared. Why do you ask?"

"I don't know. I just wondered."

Maybe I had felt embarrassed to admit my anxieties, especially to a woman, but Magda was smart enough to read into my question.

"Fear is not such a bad thing, Timo. I used to be afraid of many things: social situations, making mistakes, even just people in general. Then I studied fear, what psychologists have discovered about it. Whether you believe in God or natural selection, fear has evolved in us for our own protection. Prehistoric man used it to survive. If a dinosaur or a jealous caveman threatened him, his heart would beat faster, and he would sweat as his body prepared either to run or to fight. Our lives rarely encounter such death threatening events, and yet we still have that emotion to protect us. The problem is that we apply fear to events or things that don't threaten our lives but endanger less important aspects of our lives, like making mistakes, embarrassments, pride, and almost anything we choose. The trick is to learn how not to let fear keep you from enjoying your life, but rather to use it and to enhance it."

At first, I thought Magda was now scanning the area for a specific child, but she had been searching for an example to clarify her explanation.

"As I've said, many things used to frighten me. Sometimes they still do, but by confronting these fears and not running from them, I expand what psychologists call my 'comfort zones,' and I can enjoy life better. Let me give you an example. Remember when I told everyone about my idea of using the tunnel dirt for this children's farm?"

I nodded.

"I was nervous speaking in front of my peers."

"You didn't seem nervous."

"Trust me," she laughed a little as she spoke, "I was nervous. I used to be horrified of speaking before adult audiences. Funny, I never felt that way talking to children. When I took courses to become a teacher, several times I was forced to speak in front of my colleagues. Each time became easier. Even though I still feel a twinge of anxiety whenever I do so, I actually have learned to enjoy giving short speeches. It's become part of my comfort zone."

She glanced at her wristwatch.

"Oh, *mein Gott,* it's past time for them to clean up and take a nap."

She blew her whistle. The children formed two lines and followed her into the building.

A humming sound met me when I entered the chicken coop. Sven had used the electrical current from the security light and installed a man-sized attic fan at the tunnel entrance. It sucked in the fresh outside air and blew it throughout the tunnel making breathing easier.

After climbing down the ladder and stepping around the fan, I stood and marveled at our tunnel. It was a work of art. For two weeks I had been working with people almost five times my age, and together we had built a tunnel far more professional and durable than the Becker brothers' underpass in less time. There was enough room for me and another person to walk side-by-side beneath the sturdy wood ceiling supported by the strong support studs. Tiny drops of water landed on my arms as I passed the area we named "the rainforest," where the water main leaked from above but emptied below into Alex's clever drainage system. Farther down, I listened to the murmuring of guards in "the dead zone" above us.

Ralf nodded to me, smiled and, never seemed to tire. Without exchanging words, Gerhard and Max let me pass, and I grabbed a shovel and joined Sven pickaxing at fresh dirt beneath the West Berlin "dead zone."

For lunch, Helga had cooked a small hen for each of us. Sven called them "chicken midgets" and entertained us by making his hen dance like a hand puppet.

"We still haven't heard from Alex at the hospital," said Dora as she carved her hen with a knife and fork.

"Why don't you call the hospital and ask about Wenzel or to speak with Alex?" asked Max.

"We tried that," said Helga who finished serving and sat with us, "but they won't release any information or page Alex."

"We'll have to think of something soon. We have enough lumber through tomorrow, but that's it."

Those "midget" hens must have been loaded with vitamins, because we all seemed to have extra energy that afternoon. By the time we broke for dinner, we were a couple of meters into the area directly beneath the dead zone on the West Berlin side of the wall, almost a full day ahead of schedule.

Max excused himself from the dinner table and tried calling the hospital again.

"Still can't get any information," he said when he returned. "Timo, since we're so far ahead in the tunnel, don't come back here after you've delivered the dirt tomorrow morning. Go to the hospital instead. Find out all you can about Wenzel, but also ask Alex about where we can get more wood."

The park seemed different that night when I walked home from Max's house. With the days getting longer and the air warmer, more people walked the paths. A young couple kissed as they sat together on a park bench, the same bench where Christian's brother first tried to recruit me into the National People's Army. I stopped and sat beneath the weeping willow tree where I had slept many warm summer nights away from the stuffy apartment and my intoxicated sister and brother-in-law. It would be too chilly in a few hours to spend the night, but I had time to relax and reminisce.

When and how will I know where I stand with Martina?

Where will I be sleeping in less than a week? In the apartment? Under this tree? Somewhere in West Berlin?

Clouds rolled in and covered the stars and moonlight.

Chapter 32

Friday, May 4, 8:10 a.m.

Frieda and Horst had kept me up all night. They returned from their beer hall binge just before midnight. Horst accused Frieda of flirting, and Frieda indicted Horst for being a slob. Sometime, around two a.m., Frieda said, "We better go to bed. We have to go to work soon, and we might wake up Timo."

With just a few hours rest, I left earlier than usual to dump the dirt at the children's farm. Working without Alex would take extra time, and the forecast called for rain starting in the morning and increasing in intensity throughout the day and night. I finished just as the children started arriving at the center and raindrops sprinkled on the fresh black soil.

Fridays were the worst days to drive through East Berlin. Traffic was always heavier on that day, and the route from Glienicke/Nordbahn to Friedrichshain Municipal Hospital took me through the heart of the city. A steady, light rain accompanied me for the one-hour trip.

Wenzel had been moved to a room on the fourth floor. He shared it with two other patients. He wore an oxygen mask and raised his hand when he saw me, which alerted Alex sitting in a chair next to him and reading from a novel.

"Timo, good to see you," Alex said. He rose and greeted me.

Wenzel removed his mask and tried to say something, but Alex scolded him.

"Put that back on and don't talk. You know what the doctor said. Complete rest. I'll fill Timo in on all the details. Do you want anything, Wenzel? Timo and I are going to the cafeteria downstairs."

Wenzel shook his head, and Alex led me to the elevators. We didn't speak except for trivial chit chat.

"Is it raining now?" asked an elderly nurse in the elevator who must have noticed the damp spots on my windbreaker.

"Yes," I answered, "Light, but steady."

Alex bought two cups of coffee while I secured a table in a corner by a window, apart from others in the café.

Before Alex fully seated himself, he asked in a hushed, energetic voice, "So, how's the tunnel coming?"

I gave him the good news about our progress and Sven's attic fan idea to circulate oxygen.

"Ah, Sven. He jokes so much, sometimes we forget what a brilliant electrician's mind he possesses."

"Everyone wants to know about Wenzel's condition. Alex, why didn't you call us?"

He moved his coffee cup, so he could lean over the table and speak closer to me.

"Wenzel is doing better than expected. It wasn't a full-blown heart attack. Still, very serious, but it wasn't in his main artery. He needs complete rest for a full recovery. They sedate him every four hours." He glanced at his watch before continuing. "He's due for another sedation in less than twenty minutes. The problem is that during the first and last hours of his tranquilization, he mumbles aloud and always talks about the tunnel. I need to be here constantly to hush him or explain away his statements as something he watched on television. That's why I haven't called."

"What if he talks now while we're down here?"

Alex shook his head after sipping his coffee.

"He's fully awake right now. They allow him an hour of full consciousness between sedation sessions so he can eat, and they can ask him about his symptoms. He knows not to talk about it then.

"But, Timo, listen. I have a plan." He leaned in even closer and spoke like a little kid with a naughty idea. "They need hospital beds, and these Soviet doctors are good, but don't have any compassion for us Germans. They might release him to my care in a week. If I can convince them to release him a few days earlier, I can keep him heavily sedated, carry him through the tunnel Wednesday night as planned, and admit him to a West Berlin hospital where he can get proper care."

I nodded, but I had my doubts.

"Alex, none of us will be leaving if we don't get more lumber. We'll be fresh out by the end of today."

"Damn! I forgot about that. Let me think."

He squinted and tapped his fingers on the table as he thought. His hand slapped the tabletop, and he got up and went to the cashier. He returned with a blank sheet of paper and a pen. He spoke while writing.

"Timo, that last place we went to, where they're rebuilding the train station in Mönchmühle. Go there."

I nodded, and he looked at his watch again.

"They should still be working. Take this note to the foreman. We're old friends. It explains why I need more wood for that addition over my garage he thinks I'm building. In the meantime, I'll try to think about other construction crews and possible sites. I don't like going to the same place—"

He stopped talking when he handed me the note and looked beyond me out the window.

I turned to see what distracted him.

"They'll probably quit working for today because of the rain, so you'll have to try tomorrow. Oh, *mein Gott*," he said as he looked at his watch again and gulped down his coffee. "They'll be tranquilizing Wenzel soon. I better go. Good luck, Timo."

He left, and I sipped my coffee and listened to the rain tapping on the window behind me.

The coffee helped me stay awake during the long tedious drive in the heavy downpour and heavier traffic. It was already late afternoon when I parked the truck at Max's house. Everyone was waiting for dinner in the dining room. They had stopped working early. The loss of manpower had taken its toll on them.

I delivered the news about the lumber, Wenzel's condition, and Alex's plan to escape with us.

"I'm happy to hear that Wenzel is better, but not so glad that Alex wants to carry him through the tunnel," said Gerhard.

"Why?" asked Sven.

"Because it's risky taking an old sick man through. What if he dies? What if sneaking out of the hospital draws the attention of the authorities?" Ralf answered as if those concerns had been building inside of him, too.

Max set his beer bottle on the dining table and spoke like a wise father teaching his sons.

"My friends, I wonder if the Becker brothers had a similar discussion before they decided to leave without us."

His words silenced the conversation.

"Well," I said, "I don't think Wenzel leaving would bother anyone at the hospital. According to Alex, they're eager to whisk the patients home and make room for more."

"Tell Timo the good news," said Helga as she and Dora brought out dinner.

"Yes," added Dora as she patted Sven on the shoulders, "our old boys made some great progress today."

Max passed a plate of sausages to his right and said to me on his left, "Timo, we're right on schedule. As a matter of fact, we're a little ahead—less than a meter from the end of the dead zone. Once we get two meters beyond the barbed wire fence, we'll be behind the weeping willow trees that lined what used to be the street before they built the wall. From there, we dig straight up for two and a half meters, and we're out. We could actually leave on Tuesday instead of Wednesday if we wanted."

"*Wunderbar*," I said.

Because of the heavy rain, Ralf and Helga drove me home.

When I entered the apartment, everything hit me: the lack of sleep the night before, the long intense driving, and the heavy meal. I collapsed on the couch and fell into a dreamless slumber.

Hours later, a bold, demanding knocking on the apartment door awakened me.

Bleary eyed, I stumbled to the door and opened it.

Olaf, in his full border guard uniform, stood in the hallway.

"Is this an official visit, Olaf?"

"No, I drove straight here from my post in Boeckwitz after my guard shift. Martina is at my parents' house. They're out tonight. She wants to talk to you. Can you come with me?"

I got my jacket and left with him. It was dark, and the rain was coming down in buckets. Olaf's old beat up Trabant was parked across the street. We stood inside the glass door entrance of the building for a few minutes and waited for the downpour to let up, but it was relentless. We ducked our heads and ran while splashing in the deep curbside puddles.

I didn't think it possible that the inside of his car could look worse that the outside, but I was wrong. Piles of paper, mostly job memos and propaganda, empty plastic cups, and white bakery bags littered the passenger seat.

"Just shove those on the floor and get in," he said and got into the driver's seat.

The rain and darkness hindered visibility and made the drive slow and monotonous. We made attempts at small talk.

"Do you have to drive back to Boeckwitz tonight?"

"No, I'm off duty tomorrow. Many guards are off tomorrow because we all have to work this Sunday."

"Really? Why is that?"

He didn't answer.

We sprinted the few steps from the parked car to the front door but still managed to get drenched.

Martina sat in the rocking chair in the living room. She didn't look like the Martina I remembered. No matter what she wore or how she felt, she had always appeared beautiful to me. This night, wearing a simple blue housedress, she looked plain. Sitting in that rocker reminded me of Tante Eva rocking there last Christmas.

"Hello, Timo," she said but didn't stand or make eye contact. "Sit down, please."

"I'll be in the kitchen if you need me," Olaf said to her.

The "if you need me" part seemed odd to me, but I sat on the couch across from her.

"How have you been?" she asked.

I saw no reason for chit-chat.

"Lousy. What do you want to say?"

She looked down at her hands in her lap as she spoke.

"I understand why you're angry. I read your letter, and you're right. I owe you more of an explanation rather than just trying to avoid you, but I knew if I spoke to you again, I would have to lie to you, and I've never lied to you, Timo. I've loved you too much for that."

I just sat in silence. Whatever she had to say next must have been difficult for her because she fumbled for a full minute or so before speaking again.

"I am pregnant."

"You just said you never lied to me," I said and stood. "Remember when we left the clinic. You said you weren't having a baby."

"No, Timo. Your question made it easy for me to tell the truth. You asked' 'Are we going to be parents?' The answer is still the same. No, we are not."

"But *we* are," said Christian who entered from the kitchen. I'm sorry, Timo. Neither Martina nor I meant for this to happen."

"It's true, Timo," she said now facing me and pleading. "First, you should know that Christian's brother recruited me into the National People's Army—"

"He doesn't need to know all this," Christian interrupted.

"Yes, he does," Martina said. "He deserves to hear the whole truth. Timo, that Stasi pamphlet you saw on the kitchen table was mine. We were trying to recruit you and—"

"We? You mean you, Christian, and his brother? All those Sundays of sex were part of recruitment? When his brother threatened to have you molested like my sister? That was all a joke on me? All that time you and Christian were a couple?"

"No, it started after that party in Schönholz when we had our fight. I was all alone and sad. Christian came by and—"

"That's enough," I said.

Olaf stepped inside the living room as if preparing for me to get violent … but there was no need.

A strange numbness overtook me. It was as if all my emotions—anger, sadness, disappointment, and more—came together, cancelled each other out, and left me passive and calm. The most important aspect of this mysterious feeling was clarity.

Olaf and Christian were not a present danger, and I didn't hate Olaf. He was just a buffoon, a puppet of the state. His uniform and his job gave him the prestige that he had lacked for most of his life. Christian had killed my best friend's wife and impregnated my girl-friend—the irony of his name made me grin. The real irony was that even though I hated him, I also felt pity for this unfortunate young man who hated his job and was now trapped with a baby and a woman he could never love as much as I did.

My feelings for Martina now were much more complex. I knew a part of me still loved her and perhaps always would, but a new realization struck me, also. Maybe it wasn't new. Maybe it had always been there, but I had been hiding it from myself. We could never be happy together. Our dreams were too far apart. I would always look back on this, my first loving relationship, with fondness, but Martina no longer represented the future.

They were all part of my past now.

Before leaving, I said, "All of you spoke of 'the Soviet state of mind,' and I never quite understood what you were talking about. Now, I think I'm looking at it. I understand it, and you can have it. To hell with all of you."

Outside, the rain beat down. As the cold wetness seeped through my jacket, I felt my emotions begin to emerge from the numbness. I entered the passenger's side of Olaf's car just to escape the drenching.

My emotions exploded. I sobbed, beat the dashboard, and cursed. After a few minutes, some calm returned. I was ready to leave, but the rain hadn't let up much. To pass the time, I flicked on the overhead light, sifted through the mess of papers on the floor, and read. Most of it was propaganda and information about border guard duties. One memo stood out. It was dated earlier in the week. I couldn't believe what I was reading.

I stuffed the document into my jacket pocket and ran all the way to Max's house.

It was sometime after nine p.m. when Max put on his glasses, stood in his dining room, and read the memo aloud:

CONFIDENTIAL
30 April, 1962
On Sunday, 6 May, 1962 all Border Patrol and Border Helpers will report to assigned stations at 6 a.m. In conjunction with local GDR police and the National People's Army, thorough searches of all premises and properties located along the East Berlin border will be conducted. Any subversive materials, devises, or project activities will be secured, and residents will be arrested pending investigations.
Colonel General Erich Peter
Chief Commander of Border Troops GDR

Max tossed his glasses and the letter onto the table. He seemed to be in a trance and spoke as if he were alone and talking to himself.

"This is it. Isn't it? The end. The final disappointment. If we worked from now until Sunday, we couldn't finish the tunnel. Even if we could, we're out of wood and there's not enough time to get more."

He looked upward and said, "Why? Why, dear God? I tried to be a good man, a good servant. I attended your house every Sunday even though the government discouraged it. I worked hard and served my fellow man. I loved my wife with all my heart, but you took Hannah from me. You gave me hope for freedom after she died, for a life with her daughter and grandson when you led me to the Beckers' tunnel, and then you let them betray me. Now, this final disappointment."

In his mesmerized state, he turned and walked the few steps to the door leading into the kitchen. His fist pounded on it with each word as he asked, "Why? Why? Why? Why?"

Then he sank to his knees and wept.

I knelt next to him and put my hands on his shoulders—something he had done for me and others many times when we needed support and comfort. But I couldn't find any words of consolation. My eyes looked upward and stared at the splintering damage at the hinges he had caused with his fist to the door ... the door. That's when the idea struck me.

I spoke now as if I were under a spell.

"Stop sobbing, Max." I patted his shoulders, stood up, and asked, "Where do you keep the pencils and graph paper you used to make those tunnel sketches?"

He pointed to his work desk in the living room.

"I'm staying here tonight. You and I have some paper work to do before we go to sleep. Call the others. We're leaving tomorrow night."

Max went to the phone, and I ran to the desk.

PART V:
THE ESCAPE

Chapter 33

Saturday, May 5, 1962, 9:30 a.m.

Everyone was allowed one medium sized suitcase—one of the many details discussed during meals over the past few weeks. The basement looked like something you might see at a small airport or bus terminal with the luggage lined up at the bottom of the staircase.

Max addressed the anxious and bewildered card club members seated at his dining room table.

"I know you're all confused after my phone call last night. I used our code words 'card club is on' and said it would be this morning because, yes, we're escaping tonight. Timo brought this note that he found in his girlfriend's … his former girlfriend's brother's car."

Max read the letter aloud and received the expected reactions of horror.

Helga gasped.

"Max, please don't tell me you expect us to finish the tunnel before tomorrow. It's impossible. All that work, and for nothing," said Gerhard.

"Even if we could do it," added Ralf in his low monotone voice as he comforted Helga, "we're out of lumber and time to get it."

"All of you, calm down and listen," said Max. "I know how you feel. When I read this, I crumbled into complete despair. But Timo had a brilliant idea. We worked on it all last night. Timo, explain our plan to them."

This was unexpected. I had never addressed this group, apart from offering a quick comment or answer. I was the child, and they were the grown-ups. Except for Max and Sven, I even felt shy speaking to them in one-on-one conversations. Magda's smile caught my attention. I recalled our discussion about her similar feelings. A surge of confidence shot through me.

She nodded, and I spoke.

"Gerhard and Ralf, you're both right. There's no way we can finish the kind of tunnel we've been building and get the lumber in time. But we can finish a different kind of tunnel, a tunnel just four more meters in length in a single day. We've already done it, the Becker tunnel."

"What about the wood?" Dora and Sven asked in unison.

"I'm looking at it," I said, turned, and pointed to the kitchen door. "Max has nine standard sized doors in his house. Each door is two meters high and slightly less than a meter wide. We only need six of them to support the roof and two sides of our four-meter tunnel."

"Wait," said Gerhard "I'm picturing this in my head. Even if we build this tunnel four meters in length, we still have to dig a shaft two and a half meters upward to reach the surface."

"No, Gerhard," I said, "not if we dig at an angle."

I grabbed a large piece of brown cardboard Max had cut from a box and handed it to him. He brought it to the table and held it up. He had sketched a side view of the wall with a barbed wire fence on each side of it. The two dead zones were the areas between each fence and the wall. Below it, he had sketched our tunnel.

I drew a line from the roof of the end of our tunnel straight up to the ground level and marked it with an *x*, indicating that our tunnel now ended just inside the fence on the West Berlin side of the wall.

"Our tunnel ends two and a half meters below the surface."

My next line went from *x* straight across the ground, beneath the fence and into West Berlin. I marked the end with a *y*.

"This is where our tunnel should end. According to Max's figures, it, too, is about two and a half meters to the area beyond the line of willow trees. It's the wooded area of West Berlin that used to be a part of Tegel Forest before they cleared the land farther west to build houses."

I drew a diagonal from *y*, beneath the ground to my starting point, the roof of the end of our tunnel, and marked the connected lines *z*.

"It's a right triangle on its side," said Magda.

"Yes," I said, "and I know I'm not as educated as most of you, but I did learn some geometry in school. This longest line of the triangle I just drew is called?"

"The hypotenuse," she said.

"The hypotenuse," I repeated, "or the length of our tunnel before striking the surface. For some reason, I still remember that formula for the hypotenuse, the square root of the sums of the squares of the other two sides. It comes to a little over three and a half meters. We'll call it four meters. If we start a tunnel at the roof of the end of our present tunnel and at a forty-five-degree angle toward the surface, the width and height of the Becker tunnel, we should break into West Berlin by late tonight."

Everyone studied the diagram. So much information had been thrown at them that it took some time to absorb and to analyze it. Once they had, questions and comments flowed.

"Roots," said Ralf. "If we're digging below and beyond a line of trees and at an upward angle, we're bound to run into thick roots."

"We might avoid them. Weeping willow trees have a shallow root system," offered Gerhard. "That's why they blow down so easily in wind storms."

"We'll keep some saws and axes handy if we run into them. I can even extend the electric current that far, so we can use electric saws if we have to," said Sven.

"What about your neighbors, the Schafhausers? And what about Alex?" asked Dora.

"*Mein Gott*," said Max. "I forgot to notify them."

"I'll take care of that," Helga said and rose to her feet, "and when I call the hospital, I'll tell them it's an emergency, and I must talk with Alex. I'll just give him our code, 'the card game is on,' and hope he figures it out."

"He'll be disappointed. He counted on leaving with Wenzel," I said.

"There's something else," Helga said in confidence to Max. She spoke in his ear as if she was too embarrassed for the others to hear.

"Quiet, everyone," said Max. "Helga's brought up a good point. Most of us, because of our age, and for some of us, our size, are not as agile as we once were. This last portion of the tunnel will be small and a little tight. We'll have to crawl at an upward angle. Since the floor of it will start at about waist high, we'll use my kitchen stepstool to help us get started. But most importantly, we must help each other.

"Timo, since he is the youngest and the fittest, will go through first. He'll stay outside the hole and let us know when it's clear and safe for the next person to escape.

"Sven, can you reverse the switch on our security light, so he can operate it from just outside the hole?"

"I can't reverse it, but with wire, a high-powered battery-operated flashlight, and any kind of switch, I can rig a simple security system in a few minutes."

"Good, and if it's okay with Dora, you and I will be at the stepstool to help everyone get started, which means we'll be the last to go through."

Sven looked at Dora who nodded her approval.

"Ralf will be next," continued Max. "He's the strongest of all of us. He'll sit at the end and help pull anyone through and push them up if they have trouble."

Ralf raised his fist as a sign that he accepted his assignment.

"Max, one last question," said Gerhard. "Do you honestly think we can make it before the raid tomorrow morning?"

It was the question on everyone's mind.

Max scanned the eager faces of these people, his dearest friends, before answering.

"I've known and loved all of you much too long to lie. I'm not really sure we can do it, but we have no choice now but to try."

Sven stood on a chair and broke the silence.

"Well, why are we sitting here scratching ourselves? Let's go!"

Eager to work, we left the table. Gerhard and Ralf got busy taking doors down. Dora walked over to the Schafhauser house, and Helga called the hospital. Afterward, they would start preparing our final meals in East Berlin, God willing. Magda had called in sick at the daycare center. She became our utility worker—operating the security light, helping in the kitchen, and assisting with dirt removal. We wouldn't be taking the soil to the kids' garden, so it was unnecessary to haul it to the truck. Magda would spread it around Max's yard as if she was gardening.

I thought about how much we needed Alex's expertise as I stared at the ominous dirt wall at the end of our tunnel. Max, Sven, and I looked at it with our shovels and pickaxes in hand. It was more than just our usual digging chore. It required finesse. The new tunnel had to start from the ceiling and measure precisely a door-width-square and angle upward as close to a forty-five-degree angle as possible to reach just below West Berlin topsoil before Sunday morning.

Measuring the square was easy. Keeping the dimensions and the angle consistent was problematic. We used carpenter's tools, a sliding bevel and a bubble level to check our digging angle. Our problem? We weren't carpenters or building engineers like Alex, so it took us longer.

We worked for hours until we thought we had completed a perfectly square opening, a meter deep and at a forty-five-degree angle upward, we tried to insert the door supports.

We were off by a few centimeters. We recalculated and dug some more until the two-meter door supports fit halfway into the channel as planned. From there, the digging crept a few centimeters at a time as we edged the doors farther down the channel.

More challenges emerged. As we dug deeper, our passageway became too confined to swing a pickaxe. Our only digging tool became a pointed tip shovel. Even when Gerhard and Ralf joined us after removing all six doors from the house, just Sven and I were slim enough to use the shovel with total force and efficiency.

None of us thought or mentioned stopping to rest or to eat. By two thirty, the first set of door supports had fit all the way inside the tunnel. We had completed two meters, halfway to our destination.

"Good work, men," said Max. "Now we know we can make it, well before tomorrow. We need to stop, rest, and nourish ourselves."

Everyone agreed, and Max had to remind them not to shout their enthusiasm. Our voices might be heard above.

I sat on the floor of our new tunnel and watched them, tired but in high spirits, walk toward the entrance. I lay on my back, gazed at the door/ceiling, and imagined the West Berlin sky above me. Just for good measure, I scooted to the end and decided to dig one more shovelful of dirt before breaking to eat.

The blade hit something hard and immovable.

Chapter 34

Helga carried a plate piled high with golden brown Wiener schnitzel, and Dora followed with a steaming bowl of *Spätzle*, a kind of soft egg noodle dish.

"The first thing I'll do when I get to West Berlin is go to the best restaurant in the city and eat Schnitzel and *Spätzle* until I explode," said Max.

"I'm going to KaDeWe and shop for a week," said Helga. "I haven't seen the inside of a decent department store since they put up that damned wall."

"Me?" said Sven. "You'll find me relaxing at the sexiest strip club I can find."

"Like hell you will," Dora said and threatened to dump the bowl of *Spätzle* on his head.

I remained silent all through the meal.

Just before dessert, Max whispered to me, "You've been awfully quiet, Timo. Something wrong?"

"I need to tell you something, Max."

We went into the kitchen, and I told him about the hard object I hit with the shovel before leaving the tunnel.

"Let's go look," he said.

I crawled to the rear of the tunnel and scraped the dirt away exposing the obstacle. It reminded me of a hideous illustration, the head of Medusa, from a Greek mythology picture book I had scanned when

I was a little boy in school. But instead of a myriad of curling snakes covering her skull, a conglomeration of thick roots twisted and coiled from top to bottom.

"Damn it," said Max after he had crawled to the end and saw it.

We returned to the house.

Max broke the jovial atmosphere as the others ate cake when he announced, "As soon as you finish, get down to the tunnel. We have a problem."

Everyone took turns crawling inside to view the roots of the tree above.

"Well, on the positive side," said Gerhard, "we're almost below a weeping willow tree. Since it has a shallow root system, it means we're close to the surface. Once we get past these roots, there's no need to dig at an angle or very far. We'll be beyond the tree line and into the woods. We need only to dig about a meter more at an angle and less than a meter up, and we're out."

"If we're lucky," said Max.

"And you haven't mentioned the negative side," added Sven. "We have to cut through those thick wooden roots."

"So, let's get started," said Ralf.

"We can't use my electric reciprocating saw," said Max "Those things are as loud as jet engines. Even if there's no one in the forest, the guards in the tower will surely hear it.

Ralf grabbed a handsaw and said, "Sawing is a back and forth, not a swinging motion, so all of us, not just Timo and Sven can work."

He climbed through the tunnel.

We waited outside to hear the scraping of metal teeth cutting against the roots, but all we heard was Ralf cursing. He backed out and shook his head.

"It's useless. The saw blade is too wide to fit between those tight curving roots. Timo and Sven will have to use a hand axe and hack a top shelf at least a half meter deep before we can use the saw and cut down."

Sven and I got to work. We chopped for over an hour before we removed enough roots to start sawing. It took Ralf, Max, and Gerhard another hour and a half to saw away the exposed roots. We had only cut a half meter deep into the root system.

At that rate, it would take us ten hours without a break to reach the other side of the tree, and it was already early evening. The prospect of finishing before the Sunday morning raid seemed bleak.

"I have an idea," said Sven.

He and Max left, and I took my turn axing the roots. When my half hour shift ended, I scooted out of the channel, but no one was there. I walked back to the chicken coop where they had assembled several extension cords, Max's reciprocating saw, a couple of white bath towels, and a roll of grey duct tape. The electric saws made back then resembled machine guns seen in old American mobster movies. To operate them, you had to support the heavy metal cylindrical stock with one hand and operate the trigger on the handle. Instead of bullets coming out of the far end when you pulled the trigger, a long, sharp-toothed flexible blade moved back and forth at a blurring speed. Since the blade was no wider or longer than a steak knife, it could easily fit between the roots and cut twice as fast as the handsaw.

The problem, as Max had mentioned, was the deafening noise. Sven wrapped the body of the saw in a towel and secured it with two strips of duct tape at each end. He applied another layer of toweling over that one and fortified it with more tape.

"Ready, boys?" said Sven as he supported it on his forearm.

We covered our ears, and he pulled the trigger.

Instead of sounding like a jet plane, it sounded like a toy electric train engine. No one above the ground would detect the gentle humming.

"Alright, show me those roots," Sven said.

We each took fifteen-minute shifts operating the saw, and three hours later we had cut through all the roots. Only a meter and a half square wall of soft dark dirt stood in our way. Max and I measured the total length of our narrow tunnel.

"Just over four meters," he told the others when we emerged.

"Should we put in the door supports?" asked Ralf.

"Why waste time?" Max answered. "The tree trunk and roots over-head make a natural ceiling and the severed roots on the sides make up the walls."

"That means if we just dig about a meter horizontally and less than a meter upward, we should be out," said Gerhard.

"What are waiting for?" said Ralf. "Let's finish."

"Wait," said Sven. "We've come too far to fail because of our haste."

"Sven's right," said Max. "What time is it?"

Gerhard held his watch to the overhead lightbulb.

"It's just past ten."

"Okay," said Max, "In less than half an hour, we can dig our way out, but we don't know exactly what's on the other side in the woods. We might be right next to a footpath. There'll be a narrow but gaping hole for someone to discover even at this late hour.

"Also, we're tired, hungry, and filthy. Let's take a break. We can prepare to leave in an orderly fashion and eliminate mistakes."

We all agreed and trudged back toward the house. But if we had anticipated surprising the women with our enlightening news, they had a shock for us.

Chapter 35

Alex stood up and looked straight into Max's eyes when we entered the room. Wenzel lay on the couch with a small green tank next to him and a clear oxygen mask over his face attached with an elastic band around his head. Alex and Wenzel were dressed in suits.

Alex walked toward Max like a schoolboy approaching his teacher. At that moment, it occurred to me, and maybe to everyone, that this was Max's tunnel. We all had earned a share of it, but it was his idea, his property, his project, and his decisions were the only ones that counted.

"I'm sorry, Max. I couldn't stay here, and I couldn't leave him. Against the doctors' orders, I checked him out of the hospital. He's heavily sedated, and easy for me to carry. He'll be my responsibility. I'll check him into the best hospital in West Berlin as soon as we get out. Please, can we have our place back in line?"

Max, with deep concern in his eyes, stared at him for several seconds before he put his hands onto Alex's shoulders and spoke.

"We're not the Beckers, Alex. We don't betray our friends and neighbors.

"All of us," he addressed everyone in a louder voice, "are leaving in about an hour. Gentlemen, take turns using my shower and changing clothes. Helga, fix everyone something simple to eat and drink—no beer or alcohol, only water or coffee. We need to stay alert."

Max's words ignited a fire of action. Magda and Helga raced to the kitchen, put on aprons, and began making coffee and sandwiches. The men retrieved their luggage from the basement and searched for clean clothes and shaving kits.

"Where are the Schafhausers?" asked Max.

"They told us to alert them when we were ready. I'll go over there," Dora said and ran to the door.

Holidays hadn't meant much to me while living with my sister, but this flurry of activity sparked a vague childhood memory of Christmas morning when my parents were alive.

The thrill of escape trumped our fatigue. Helga made *Leberkäse* (a sort of meatloaf made of beef, pork, bacon, and onions) and egg sandwiches that we ate while preparing to leave, and Magda delivered cups of coffee.

Since I had come straight to Max's the night before from Martina and Olaf's house, I had no clean clothes or luggage. All the men provided me with some fresh garments from their luggage, and Max gave me a large canvas sack for baggage.

Sven showered and changed first so he could work on rigging the flashlight, wire, and switch into a signal system.

At around 11:10 p.m., Max gave the first order.

"Timo and Sven, go now and finish the dig. Take your time. I'll organize everyone here. By the time you finish, we should be crammed inside the chicken coop and ready to go."

Sven and I, shovels in hand, marched through the tunnel, with luck, for the last time. Taking turns, within a half hour, we had dug a cave a little more than a meter deep beyond our passageway supported by doors and tree roots. It didn't matter that our new cave had no roof support. We'd be removing that dirt anyway. If our calculations were correct, fresh West Berlin air waited less than a meter above us.

I turned the shovel blade skyward and knocked some loose soil above. Sven scooped the fallen earth out of the crawlspace. My hand slithered like a snake upward and through the dirt, but my fingertips didn't feel any air. After more digging, I could almost stand up in the cave. I dug my hand into the dirt ceiling again and felt only dirt ... and then something else, something damp and coarse.

I grabbed a handful and yanked it down. Sven and I gazed at it as if we had discovered precious gems. It was grass—just a common lump of green filthy West Berlin sod, but it symbolized freedom to us.

"Come on. Let's finish the job," said Sven.

Within ten minutes we had dug a shoulder-width hole above us. I peeked up and saw a cluster of stars in the sky. Standing straight up would expose my head above our opening. We figured we were just inside the narrow strip of wooded area, once a part of Tegel Forest, but nothing was certain. I could have been poking my head into someone's backyard, by a city street, or even just outside the barbed wire fence of the dead zone and in full view of the border guards in the watchtower.

When I locked my knees, my eyes and nose rose above the grass line. Total darkness shrouded my head as I looked in the direction of the wall. The tree trunk and the low hanging weeping willow branches shielded me like a curtain cut into hanging strips. Through the hanging strips, I could see the border guard standing in the watchtower, but there was no way he could see me. In the opposite direction, a streetlamp about sixty or seventy meters away illuminated a tiny section of the narrow forestry land.

"Sven, give me a little boost," I said as if I didn't want to awaken a sleeping bear.

He cupped his hands around my heel, and I stepped up until I could force myself out of the hole with my arms and sat. The streetlamp beam exposed a portion of a paved footpath through the woods. I crawled in the other direction toward the leafy hanging branches and peered into the lighted dead zone and up at the watchtower. To my surprise, only one guard stood watch in the tower. Normally, there were at least two or more.

Sven's head protruded from the hole when I edged back. We crept back to the standing portion of our tunnel and spoke in whispers.

"It's perfect, Sven. When each person comes out of the hole, we'll be in total darkness. There's a footpath beneath the streetlamp. We can direct them toward it, and they're out. One thing puzzles me."

"What?"

"There's only one guard in the tower. Why?"

Sven contorted his face and shook his head. "I don't know, but it's to our advantage. Maybe the good Lord is with us now. Anyway, let's go tell Max and the others."

Max and Ralf stood by the ladder at the bottom of the entrance shaft when we approached them and told them the situation.

"Why do you think there's only one guard in the tower?" I asked.

"My guess," said Max, "is that they're using all available police and military personnel for the raid that should start," he paused to look at his watch, "in less than five hours.

"Ralf, go with them. When you three are all set up, Sven, come down and let me know. Whenever Timo gives us the signal—remember, one light means all clear; two flashes mean stop—we'll start sending people through. Sven and I will help them get started at the beginning of the crawlspace. Ralf will pull them through and push them up and out if they need help. I'll line the others up now and tell them to head for the lighted path. Timo will direct them once they're out. Any questions?"

We stared at each other in silence. In the dim lighting, we looked dreamlike, almost like ghosts. It was hard to believe that after all the time, work, frustrations, and planning, it would all be over in a few minutes. Our lives were about to change forever.

"Then good luck," Max said, and we headed through the tunnel.

Ralf positioned himself, seated, at the bottom of the exit shaft. He held the flashlight pointed down the crawlspace. Sven had attached a wire from the on/off switch of the flashlight to a small pushbutton switch that he had taped to a transistor radio. Cheap transistor radios were popular among teens back then, so I looked perfectly natural holding it. All I had to do is push the button, and it would all start.

Who would be the first to come through? Would they make it? Is this all really happening or just a dream?

It was near midnight. Quiet. No one was in sight or on the path. The border guard in the tower focused all his attention toward the east side of the wall.

I pressed the button.

I had expected to see a large, dark piece of luggage protruding from the hole.

Instead, Alex's head popped up. That made perfect sense. Max envisioned the tunnel, but Alex engineered it. Since Max chose to be last, Alex should be first. The absence of luggage seemed logical, also. His baggage would be Wenzel.

I positioned my forearms beneath his armpits and pulled him up, and Ralf pushed from below. This became our standard routine for everyone. As soon as Alex was out, he reached back into the hole and waited to grab Wenzel.

Wenzel, in a semi-conscious state, mumbled like a drunk as Sven and Max pushed, and Ralf pulled his deadweight body through the channel. Before we tugged him up, I mimed directions to Alex: cover Wenzel's mouth, carry him toward the streetlamp, but wait until I check the guard's activity.

After much effort, we lifted Wenzel out. Alex cradled him and waited while I checked on the guard who seemed to watch both sides of the wall. After nearly a minute, he seated himself and focused east.

I signaled Alex to go.

He nodded a farewell, turned, and plodded with his beloved partner in tow toward the light. Alex stood for a moment on the trail. He looked one last time toward the wall, then disappeared into the darkness.

We had done it.

It was my job to keep the line moving. I crept toward the curtain of branches and rechecked on the guard. He continued his watch in the other direction, the east—where escapes started and ended with murder in the dead zone. I maneuvered my way back to the hole and felt for my transistor radio/signal switch. Just before pressing the button to initiate the next escape, two people, not Alex and Wenzel, appeared under the lamp post. The young couple, maybe in their late teens or early twenties, stopped, embraced, and kissed as if the artificial brightness was moonlight.

A sadness overtook me. The sight reminded me of my romantic moments with Martina, all that I had cherished, all that I would miss. But a new thought struck me. What new love adventures waited for me in West Berlin?

I waited for the couple to stop kissing and move on, but they had other ideas. Instead of continuing down the path, they walked in my direction. I scooted closer to the tree trunk, so the hanging branches hid me. The rustling of dead debris beneath their feet got louder and louder as they got closer.

This time, I hit the button twice.

The crunching stopped. Soft murmuring, the way people talk late at night in total darkness, followed. I had expected the willow tree branches to part like a hanging rope door and the couple to enter my shrouded area for a session of love-making, but they chose the tree next to me, probably because it was farther away from the guard tower and the searchlight.

Still, it was too close. They couldn't be nearby during our escape.

I waited and listened.

The awkward task of removing clothing in the dark must have created the laughing and shuffling noises followed by the groaning and moaning of heated sex. Their lovemaking built to a crescendo, and then faded into silence.

I hoped that now that they had consummated their romantic evening, they would move on, but no, they stayed. Maybe they had planned to stay all night.

Something had to be done. The others must have been going mad wondering why I hadn't signaled for the next getaway. If I waited for the couple to leave, it might be light, or worse, the scheduled Sunday morning raid might start.

An idea struck me. My unknown presence had been working against me. I clicked the on/off disc switch on the transistor radio. It worked, so I tuned it to a popular rock and roll station that broadcast from West Berlin. Everyone in East and West Germany had been talking about a new group, The Beatles, who performed in Hamburg. They were a backup band for rock and roll singer Tony Sheridan. Sheridan had let them record a cut on his latest album, and the song became a rage on radio stations all over Europe. I turned the volume up and sang along, just loud enough for them, but not the guard to hear:

"Ain't she sweet?
See her walking down the street.
Well, I ask you very confidentially,
Ain't she sweet?
Just cast a light ... "

"Shit!" a male voice shouted followed by the shuffling sounds of people dressing in the dark.

More than the worry of him coming over and beating me, I dreaded them discovering the hole, maybe even stepping into it, and alerting the guard. But they decided just to get dressed and leave.

Their romantic interlude spoiled, they headed down the lighted path and vanished.

I flashed the all clear signal again.

Chapter 36

Gerhard, Magda and Dora followed. Sven insisted that Dora leave with the couple. He would meet up with her later at Dicke Wirtin, an historic all-night pub in West Berlin. Ralf and I maneuvered Dora and Magda out, and they waited for Gerhard under the tree. As he climbed up, I checked on the guard whose primary concern was the east side dead zone. I turned to signal them to leave, but something disturbed me. I crawled on my knees toward them and spoke in a hushed voice.

"He's focused in the other direction and not likely to turn around, but if he does and sees three adults crossing the field with bulging travel bags, he'll wonder where they came from."

"Timo is right," Gerhard said and laid his hand on my shoulder. "You ladies go first. Wait for me somewhere down the path."

The women agreed, and Gerhard and I crawled toward the curtain of branches to spy on the guard. As I parted the hanging leafy twigs, Gerhard spoke to me in a way I had never heard him address me before. He was an intellect. My impression was that he thought of me as this undereducated kid who would be doing menial labor jobs the rest of his life.

"Timo, Magda told me that she has had some interesting conversations with you when you delivered the dirt to her daycare center."

I nodded but kept my attention on the guard.

"I, too, have listened and watched you," he continued. "I think you are a bright young man with possibly a great future." He returned his hand to my shoulder and said, "Should you ever need anything from us in West Berlin, don't hesitate to ask. We'd love to help you."

I turned toward him and said, "*Danke,* Dr. Lehrs. Now, join the others. They need you."

He clasped my hand with both of his and dashed off.

A bulging brown leather valise jutted up the hole, and I grabbed it. I hadn't recognized it because it wasn't with the stacked luggage in Max's basement. It belonged to the Schafhausers. *Frau* Schafhauser wore a short skirt and a dark sleeveless top, not exactly tunnel-crawling attire. As soon as I pulled her out, she reached back into the hole. A minute later, she pulled her German shepherd pup out. The dog seemed frightened and confused. I worried about it barking or making some noise that might alert the guard, but it calmed down in Frau Schafhauser's arms.

We waited a few minutes until I was sure the guard had focused his attention toward the east side of the wall, before I signaled them to leave.

That left five of us: Helga, Ralf, Sven, Max, and me.

Helga wanted to be last. She harbored the same fear as with the Becker tunnel. She felt she was too big to fit through the narrow passageway, but there was something more she and Ralf had kept from all of us.

"I have claustrophobia. I panic in small tight spaces," she had confessed to Max when Sven and I were finishing the dig.

"You'll be fine," Max had reassured her. "It's not like the Becker crawlspace. Ours is only four meters long. You'll close your eyes and put your arms in front of you. At the same time as Sven and I are pushing your legs, you'll feel your husband's hands pulling you through. You'll be out in seconds. Trust me.

"We'll let the Schafhausers go ahead of you. Then you, Ralf, Sven, Timo, and I will join Dora, Gerhard, and Magda in West Berlin for a victory beer."

Helga agreed.

Max embraced her, but felt his hands sweat with fear after thinking about Helga's confession.

I had given the all clear signal at least three times, but neither a person nor a suitcase came through the hole. After about fifteen minutes, I peeked down the shaft. Ralf wasn't there. I climbed back through the crawlspace.

Helga sat on her luggage and cried.

"I can't do it. I just can't do it," said Helga between sobs.

Ralf held his wife and said, "It's okay, Helga. I'll help them through, and then we'll go back."

"Wait," said Max. "I have an idea."

He walked toward the tunnel entrance and returned minutes later with a glass of water and something in his other hand.

"Here, take these," he said, dropped two capsules into Helga's hand, and handed her the tumbler of water. "The doctor gave these to Hannah a few years ago when she worried herself sick over her daughter's rough pregnancy. They're tranquilizers. They won't put you to sleep, but they might calm you down."

Helga took them, and we waited about ten or fifteen minutes.

She took a deep breath and said, "I'm okay now. I'm ready to go."

Ralf got into position, and I, pushing their suitcase, followed. After giving the all clear signal, I waited over the hole.

No one can say for sure what happened next, but this is my theory. Helga stretched out in the passageway, and Max and Sven pushed her forward. She was halfway through, her upper body in the tree root section and her lower body in the part supported by the doors. When she pulled her knees up to crawl forward, her rear end hit the top door, and she panicked. She tried to stand up and raised it. One or both side doors fell inward, and a full two-meter length of tunnel collapsed. Ralf grabbed her hands and yanked her through the rest of the way. I pulled her up, and the two of them were out in a split second. They ran to the light and left their luggage behind.

I parted the weeping willow branches and peered into the dead zone. The ground had caved into a hole that looked like an open grave. Max and Sven climbed out of it and found themselves caught above the grave and in the dead zone, this area between the fence was still considered East Berlin. They ran toward the barbed wire fence. The guard was not in the tower. He was coming down the ladder to investigate. With luck, my help, and enduring some painful cuts, they might make it through the razor-sharp barbs before the guard could level his weapon and shoot them.

"Halt," said the guard.

At first, I thought it was Christian. How appropriate that he be the guard who would spoil our escape—the man who killed Max's wife and impregnated my girlfriend. But it wasn't him. This guard was older. He must have been my age when the Soviets took us over. What were his feelings about that? What possessed him to become a border guard? Who was he, really? All night long, I watched a soldier, not a man, just something inside a uniform doing a job from a watchtower.

Sirens whined in the distance. Soon more guards, guns, and bright lights would flood the dead zone where Max and Sven must have tripped an alarm system.

Beneath the shade of his hat and the guise of his uniform, the tall guard looked intimidating. His rigid, tight jaws made him appear tough, but his eyes, wide open and unblinking, revealed the face of a frightened man. The barrel of his weapon shook. He was positioned and justified by East German law to execute two criminals because they were in the dead zone. But why hadn't he?

"Down on the ground, young man," he said to me.

That's why. I could be hit by the gunfire. That's what the West German government and the western world waited for—a person outside the dead zone on the West Berlin side to be shot by a border guard. That would give the rest of the world a reason to tear down the wall and apply international law against the Soviet Union.

"No," I said.

"Lie down!" he repeated.

"You'll have to shoot me, too."

Max, his hands in the air, looked at me with both pride and sadness in his eyes. One would have expected a man in his situation to be frightened or hysterical. Not Max Thomas. He knew he had done his best. He was resigned to his fate.

"Do as he says, Timo. It's no use. He can separate us at any time and kill us anyway. You have a life to live. Remember, we found freedom for ten people. Maybe this is God's way of ending life for me and Sven. If we must die, we may as well go as martyrs ... like his son."

Sven nodded in agreement.

I dropped to my knees but didn't even bother to hide my thoughts and feelings.

"God's way? God's way, Max? Who is this God you talk of, pray to, and worship every Sunday? What kind of God ..."

But that's all I could get out. My anger and despair choked me, and I buried my head in my arms and waited.

Two torrents of gunfire crackled overhead.

My head raised into the thin cloud of grey smoke. As the smolder lifted, I expected to see the bloody corpses of my two best friends, but no ... Max and Sven still stood tall. The guard had shot at the ground.

"Pull back on the barbed wire, young man and let your friends step over and then under," he ordered above the sound of sirens becoming louder and louder. "Hurry, before more guards get here."

We followed his instructions.

The sirens screamed at a deafening pitch from the other side of the wall, and then ceased.

We stood on the West Berlin side and stared at him in awe.

"Get out of here. All of you. I'll be in enough trouble as it is without proof that I let three Germans escape."

Max and Sven ran toward the footpath.

I waited a few moments before saying, "*Danke*, but why didn't you kill them?"

"Technically, they are still in East Berlin on this side of the fence, but in my mind, they made it to the West. I'm neither an East German nor a West German ... I'm a German. Now, turn away and run. Your dreams are calling you."

I followed his advice and never set eyes on the Berlin Wall again until November 9th, 1989 when I watched it crumble to the ground on television.

Chapter 37

Alex took Wenzel to Lazarus Hospital where he recovered from his heart attack. The two men moved into an apartment within the growing gay community in a section of West Berlin. Hamburg, the former center for homosexuals, had cracked down and enforced new anti-gay laws, and many fled to other big West German cities, including West Berlin.

I wish the story of Alex and Wenzel ended happily-ever-after, but it wasn't so. In an ironic twist, Alex died of a rare undetected disease within a year. Wenzel found it difficult to survive without his loving partner and committed suicide in the spring of 1965.

Magda and Gerhard Lehrs settled in Steglitz, within the American sector of West Berlin. Gerhard hopped on his bicycle two days a week and rode to The Free University of Berlin where he taught as an adjunct professor in the Department of Humanities. A group of professors and students who broke away from Humboldt University, the institution in East Berlin that had fired Gerhard for his liberal views, founded The Free University of Berlin in West Berlin in 1948 to seek academic freedom. His colleagues welcomed him with opened arms, and he enjoyed the respect and prestige of being a top literary intellect.

Many families of American soldiers stationed in West Berlin during the Cold War lived in Steglitz, also. Magda tutored American children and ran a babysitting service from their new home, a two-bedroom duplex with a patio and a small fenced-in yard.

The Schafhausers and their dog, Bach, vanished. No one ever heard from them again—not even a "*Danke.*"

The Seilers, Ralf and Helga, lived for a while with Ralf's cousin in a small apartment just north of West Berlin's central train station, now called Europaplatz. They moved a few years later to Munich and resided across the street from Hundskugel, the oldest restaurant in Munich.

Helga harbored guilt for almost getting Max and Sven killed, despite their words of forgiveness and consolation, until her dying day in the winter of 1972.

Ralf lived another seven years and died of old age.

Freedom set well with Sven and Dora. It energized them and rekindled their youth. They embraced West Berlin's nightlife, made friends, and later relocated to Hamburg, Germany's renowned club scene center. A little too old to frequent the erotic bars on the Reeperbahn or raucous nightclubs like The Star Club where the Beatles played, they found a bar a few blocks away that catered to adults within their age group. Dora worked part-time as a waitress, and Sven made himself welcome there by telling jokes, performing simple magic tricks, and fixing things.

Sven and Dora lived life to the fullest. That's the way I remembered them. I neither learned nor had a desire to learn how, when, or where they passed on.

Max didn't stray far from his house or chicken coop on the other side of the wall. As planned, he lived in Frohnau with his stepdaughter, her husband, and their infant son. Just as freedom nourished the youth in Sven and Dora, raising a grandson invigorated Max. He taught him all the valuable things about life that he had taught me: patience, caring, respect, tenacity, empathy, faith, forgiveness, and much, much more. Guiding a child into adulthood kept Max alive. That was his gift to both me and his grandchild. Our maturity was all he needed in return.

Max lived 101 years.

And me? What about Timo Fuerst?

Max's new family invited me to stay with them until I could find work and somewhere to live. After ten days of a futile job search, I lied and told them I had landed a job as a delivery boy and had an apartment in the city. The economic growth rate in West Berlin had slowed down following the building of the wall. More and more people came to the city—some curious to see the Berlin Wall, some just curious. West Berlin became a bustling, overcrowded, but an exciting center for young people. Jobs, however, were scarce.

I couldn't impose on the hospitality of Max's family or their bonding relationship forever, so I lied and left.

The summer of 1962 marked my poorest period but created some of my fondest memories. Sleeping under trees in beautiful parks had been part of my young life in Glienicke/Nordbahn, so West Berlin's over 500 acre urban park, Tiergarten, became my comfortable summer residence. Berliners called it their "green lung." I shared the winding tree-lined paths and open green spaces with many older teens and young adults who became my neighbors and friends. We shared everything: food, money, clothes, odd job information, and life stories.

As summer came to an end, so did my carefree attitude. I worried about what I would do for work and a place to live. Remembering his last words before running to freedom, "Should you ever need anything from us in West Berlin, don't hesitate to ask," I "borrowed" an unlocked bicycle parked at the train station and peddled to Steglitz for a visit with Gerhard and Magda.

The Lehrs took pity on my plight and offered me space in their extra bedroom, rent free, but under certain conditions. I had to promise to finish my secondary schooling, find part-time work, help around the house, and return the stolen bicycle.

This became the turning point in my life. With Gerhard's academic influence, the Lehrs enrolled me in the local Gymnasium, the highest form of secondary school in Germany. Gymnasiums were comparable to American prep schools. No doubt, the academic demands exceeded my intellect, but with Magda's tutoring, I made it through and scored high on my *Abitur* (the standard final exam). During that time, she counseled me, "You have inventive ideas for beautifying and improving Berlin and other German cities with parks and playgrounds, and I've seen some of your sketches, Timo. Did you know there is a career in that? It's called civil engineering. There are schools all over the world for that. You've learned English very well. If you applied and were accepted to one in America, you could obtain a student visa that paved a path for your dreams."

After graduating from the Polytechnic Institute of Brooklyn, I landed a job working for the City of New York Department of Parks and Recreation as an intern and later as a full-fledged civil engineer. I married, moved across the river to nearby New Milford, New Jersey where we raised our son, Maximilian Thomas Fuerst.

Epilogue

"Dad, Dad, you fell asleep while watching TV again. Wake up, Dad," he says and shakes the shoulders of his father.

Timo opens his eyes to the real world. He has been reliving his past in dreams, and his segue into reality is slow and somewhat confusing. At first, he sees himself as his son who rouses him to consciousness.

"Dad, it's after eleven thirty, past Gina's curfew. She stayed here too long. I know I just got my license, and you and Mom don't want me driving at night, but can I please drive her home? I'll come right back. Promise."

Gina stands behind Max and near the front door. Neither her physique nor her attire suggests the look of Martina, and yet, something about her reminds Timo of his first love.

The opened front door reminds him of something else. Yes, the tunnel, the Thomas tunnel, built as tall as a doorway so you could walk proud and upright into the future.

He is fully conscious now and back in the present. He reaches into his pocket, pulls out a set of keys and tosses it to his son.

"Turn away and run. Your dreams are calling you."

Max glances back at his girlfriend, and they exchange a silent laugh.

"Sure, Dad."

Before young Max closes the door behind them, Timo hears his son say, "Don't mind the old man. Sometimes I think he came from a different world."

They disappear into the darkness.

Author's Final Note

I visited Berlin for the first time in 1995. One sight intrigued me—The Checkpoint Charlie Museum. Today, many trip advisors might call it a tourist trap. For me, it was the catalyst for this book.

The museum chronicles with documents, photos, and authentic exhibits, every attempt made to go under, over, around, and through the Berlin Wall from 1961 to 1989. In that time, 3.5 million people escaped East Germany to the West, many via Berlin, and over 100 lost their lives trying. Of all the fascinating exhibits, one tiny blurb about a little-known tunnel constructed by a group of senior citizens from a northern East Berlin suburb captivated me.

As soon as we returned home, my research began. I spent hours at Chicago's Harold Washington Library and uncovered several translated journal articles. This was one of the most comprehensive pieces:

> West Berliners were heartened by accounts of unique and successful flight attempts, such as the one described below. East Germans used ingenious methods to escape, digging tunnels under the Wall, ramming reinforced vehicles through border crossings, swimming across lakes or rivers with the help of diving equipment, or flying across the border in homemade hot air balloons.

"It Couldn't Go on Like that Any Longer!"
The Flight of the Seventy-Year-Olds

Of all the daring undertakings through which people from the [Soviet] zone and East Berlin have managed to escape to freedom time and again – despite all the barriers and the violent measures of Soviet zonal authorities – this must be among the most astonishing: through arduous work, twelve elderly people managed to dig a tunnel under the zonal border in the northern section of Berlin and fled through it to West Berlin. The group was led by an 81-year old man from Glienicke; he owned a piece of land and his own hauling company there. Most of the other men involved are about 70 years old. A 16-year-old boy joined the group only on the last day.

It is truly indicative of conditions in the Zone State that even elderly people, whose material livelihood is assured and who have been inwardly rooted in their immediate surroundings for decades, decide to flee. Anyone who knows what it means for a family like that of refugee Max Thomas to leave the business they owned for forty-one years, their house and garden, and risk their lives, can appreciate the kind of pressure that people in Ulbricht's SED-state live under. Yesterday, the refugees were introduced at a press conference hosted by the Berlin [Political] Prisoners' Circles; when the 81-year-old Thomas was asked why he took the hardship and the danger of the flight upon himself, he replied, "Because we wanted to get to freedom. It couldn't go on like that any longer. I don't even want to be buried over there when I die."

The tunnel that the seven men, the four women, and the 16-year-old climbed out of on May 5th in Frohnau, on this side of Oranienburger Chaussee, which forms the zonal border there, has since been discovered, five days after the escape, by the "People's Police." The home of Max Thomas, in whose henhouse the tunnel began, is now occupied by the People's Police.

The refugees reported that they worked on the tunnel for sixteen days. The two 70-year-old men removed almost 4,000 pails of dirt and carried them to a shed 80 feet away; all the while, Max Thomas pretended to be working in the garden and warned the workers whenever a People's Police patrol approached. Since a border patrol passed the house on Oranienburger Chaussee about every fifteen minutes, work had to be constantly interrupted. Nevertheless, according to their reports, the families were in very high spirits. The women described how they brought their husbands beer and cooked for them. There was never any "moment of crisis" in which they wanted to abandon their efforts.

The entrance to another tunnel through which 28 people successfully fled to the West in January was only four houses down from Max Thomas's house. Back then, the elderly people who knew of the escape plan were left behind, because it was feared that they would be a hindrance.

The twelve elderly people completed their work with particular thoroughness. They created a passageway through which they could walk almost completely upright: at some points it was 1.75 meters high. It was 32 meters long. When asked why they built the tunnel so high, which made their work so much harder, they gave an astonishing answer: "We and our wives wanted to walk comfortably and unbowed into freedom."

(Source: C. Gennrich, "„Es ging so nicht mehr weiter! "Die Flucht der Siebzigjährigen" ["„It Couldn't Go on Like That Anymore! "The Flight of the Seventy-Year-Olds"], Tagesspiegel, May 19, 1962. Translation: Allison Brown)

Further investigation uncovered a disturbing fact. The Becker tunnel, four houses down the block ("… *the elderly people who knew of the escape plan were left behind, because it was feared that they would be a hindrance.*") received worldwide attention. Several books and magazine articles chronicled the Beckers' escape. An international film starring American actor Don Murray entitled *Escape from East Berlin* and *Tunnel 28* premiered all over the world including the United States in the fall of 1962 and the winter of 1963, but no one seemed to follow up the daring escape of Max Thomas and company with a book or a movie.

My extensive digging uncovered these few pictures which later became part of the *Fluchttunnel Glienicke* website dedicated to three tunnel escapes from Glienicke/Nordbahn:

Max Thomas (wearing the hat) and his fellow escapees in West Berlin.
Photo courtesy of Torsten Dressler M.A.
Geschäftsinhaber/ Archäologe.

The chicken coop entrance.
Photo courtesy of Torsten Dressler M.A.
Geschäftsinhaber/ Archäologe.

Entrance shaft.
Photo courtesy of Torsten Dressler M.A.
Geschäftsinhaber/ Archäologe.

Inside the tunnel.
Photo courtesy of Torsten Dressler M.A.
Geschäftsinhaber/ Archäologe.

My name must be added to the list of people who overlooked Max Thomas and his remarkable feat in history. After gathering the sparse information and pictures from the escape, I filed all of it in a manila folder and forgot about it for twenty years.

Dorinda, my wife, and I, along with another couple, returned to Berlin in 2015. One particularly new attraction struck me, The Berlin Wall Memorial. It contains the last piece of the Berlin Wall with the preserved grounds around it and extends 1.4 kilometers along the former border strip. The moment I viewed the wall, all my enthusiasm for the Thomas tunnel resurfaced. The following day, I excused myself from an outing with the others and bought a roundtrip ticket to Frohnau, the West Berlin suburb where the Thomas tunnel ended.

As soon as I stepped from the Frohnau train station, I realized why Max Thomas chose to live his final years there. It might be the most beautiful little town I have ever seen.

The main street, Edelhofdamm, is a two-way road separated by a wooded area shading a walking path similar to the Tegel Forest path in the story. The path ended where the Berlin Wall once separated Frohnau from the Thomas house in Glienicke/Nordbahn. Now, it's B/96, a two-lane highway.

This is the wooded area and path where the escapees emerged into the West Berlin suburb:

On the parkway, not far from where Max Thomas had lived, stands a memorial, three posts: a three-meter high structure symbolizing the height and position of the original wall and two upright posts in memory of escape fatalities.

This organic food store occupies the former Thomas property:

CPSIA information can be obtained
at www.ICGtesting.com
Printed in the USA
BVHW080731090220
571842BV00002B/115